Rain & Fire

A Companion to the
LAST DRAGON CHRONICLES

Also by Chris d'Lacey

The Last Dragon Chronicles

The Fire Within

Icefire

Fire Star

The Fire Eternal

Dark Fire

Fire World

The Fire Ascending

The Dragons of Wayward Crescent

Gruffen

Gauge

RAIN
&
FIRE

A Companion to the
LAST DRAGON CHRONICLES

CHRIS AND JAY D'LACEY

ORCHARD BOOKS ◆ NEW YORK
AN IMPRINT OF SCHOLASTIC INC.

Library of Congress Cataloging-in-Publication Data

d'Lacey, Chris.
Rain & fire : a companion to the last dragon chronicles / Chris and Jay d'Lacey. —
1st Scholastic ed.
p. cm.
ISBN 978-0-545-41453-1
1. d'Lacey, Chris. Last dragon chronicles — Handbooks, manuals, etc. 2. Fantasy
fiction, English — History and criticism — Handbooks, manuals, etc. 3. Children's
stories, English — History and criticism — Handbooks, manuals, etc. I. d'Lacey, Jay.
II. Title.
PR6104.L27Z58 2012
823'.92 — dc23
2012014374

10 9 8 7 6 5 4 3 2 1   12 13 14 15 16

Printed in the U.S.A.   23
First Scholastic edition, October 2012

For Professor Robert Jahn, Brenda Dunne —

Hug and Hum

(Nice to know we're not the only scribblers in the

Margins of Reality . . .)

. . . and with grateful thanks to all the crew in LR, BX,

and NJ: You know who you are — wom!

CONTENTS

Stories float around like snowflakes, don't they? They settle on the ears of anyone who'll listen.

— *Zanna (from* Fire Star)

Hello, and a warm welcome to you all. *Hrrr!*

Packed within these covers is a huge amount of information about Chris d'Lacey, his life as an author, and his fantasy series, the Last Dragon Chronicles. As his wife and business partner, I can assure you that what you discover herein is accurate and authentic, and much of it is material that you will not be able to find elsewhere — but this is no dry academic textbook to be pored over in some dark and dusty tower. This is a book that can be read from start to finish, like any other, but equally it can be opened at random — for wherever you dip in, you will find snippets of information to hold your attention, anecdotes to make you laugh, or background history to share with your friends.

This, then, is the inside story of the Last Dragon Chronicles, including:

The Fire Within
Icefire
Fire Star
The Fire Eternal
Dark Fire
Fire World
The Fire Ascending

Jay d'Lacey, Brixham, 2012

Imagine you are a young man, twenty years old and just starting out on a journey of independence. You want to leave home to go to college and earn a degree in . . . let's say Geography. You apply to a number of schools and you're happily accepted by a small college with a decent reputation.

Then having found your place of learning you need to arrange some accommodation. There are no dormitories at the college itself, so you need to apply to one of the halls of residence nearby. However, because you've been slow to read the paperwork (or more likely misplaced it), all the halls are full. Lectures begin in a few days' time. You need to find somewhere else to stay — and fast.

So waving good-bye to your hometown, Blackburn, you hop onto a train and head southeast. Where you're going is a fair old distance away. You'll probably fall asleep with your nose against the window and snore, to the annoyance of everyone in the train car. Fortunately, you're in no danger of missing your stop because the train ends in Boston, where you have to change. Time for a sandwich and a cup of coffee while you wait on a short, fairly isolated platform for your connection into the suburbs.

The train that arrives is nothing like the express that brought you this far. It's a little dingy (inside and out). It rattles. The train cars move like a broken concertina. The people in the cars talk with a different accent from yours and none of them seem to be in any kind of hurry. The same could be said of the train itself. It stops every few minutes at stations that are becoming ever more rural. The busy streets of Boston have given way to green fields, low stone walls, and trees. It's autumn, so the leaves are turning russet and brown, but most of them are clinging to their branches for now. You

4

see churches, parks, the occasional stretch of water. Narrower roads. Old-fashioned telephone booths. People wobbling around on bicycles. The houses are redbrick, clustered into rows. One of these is going to be your destination.

When the train finally pulls in, the only person to get off is you. Slinging your one bag over your shoulder, out through the turnstile you go.

From a grubby little man at a newsstand on Main Street, you buy the afternoon edition of the *Scrubbley Evening Echo*. You flip to the pages listing places to rent. What you see there doesn't look good. Everywhere is *incredibly* expensive. The paltry wad of bills you've stashed in your wallet is now cowering somewhere deep in your pocket. It would barely fund a week in any of these places. All you would be able to afford to eat would be a can of soup — and you'd have to make it last. Just to make matters worse, a lively autumn breeze lifts the paper from your fingers and carries it down the length of Main Street. It flies into the face of a large black Doberman. The dog doesn't look pleased. You decide to move on.

As you stroll up Main Street, you come to an opening between the rows of shops. A civic center of some sort, with a large white building at the far end. Beyond it you can see a huddle of trees. You feel drawn to go and look at them. *Powerfully* drawn, but you don't know why. Right beside you is a signpost, complete with blue signs. The big white building turns out to be a library. The trees are the Scrubbley Library Gardens. You stare into the grounds, looking slightly lost. Strangely, you feel as if you've only just awoken. As if everything that has gone before simply doesn't matter. As if nothing even existed before this day.

"Hello. Are you lost?" A little old lady with a shopping cart is tugging your sleeve.

"I'm, erm, looking for . . . tourist information," you say, noting there's a blue sign indicating that it's up

Main Street. The old lady points in the opposite direction. But then, old ladies are like that sometimes.

The Tourist Information Center is a yellow stone building at the intersection of roads leading out of town. Perhaps they can provide you with a list of places known for student accommodation. Well, they might if they were open. It's Wednesday afternoon. Half-day closing. Your shoulders sag. This adventure is not going well.

Sighing, you sit down on the steps of the closed TIC with your bag upon your knees and your chin upon your bag. People pass. They look at you. They smile. They wonder, perhaps, if you should have a cap for donations by your feet and a wire-haired dog on a blanket beside you. The thought of hanging a sign around your neck saying GOOD HOME WANTED does pass through your mind, just as a post office van pulls up nearby. Idly, you watch the postman unlock the mailbox and scoop the cascading letters into a sack. He locks the mailbox up again and throws the sack of letters into the van. Then he roars off into the countryside.

That's when you see that he's missed a letter. It's in the gutter at the foot of the mailbox, in danger of being run over by dozens of car tires. So, hauling your bag onto your shoulder once more, you step into the road and pick up the letter. This will be your token good deed for the day. *Tink*. Back into the mailbox it goes. Bye-bye, letter. Have a nice journey. You shrug and turn around. This random act of kindness has left you standing outside another newsstand. Nothing special about that, you think. But in the newstand is a board full of flyers. Right away, your eye is drawn to this:

HOUSING AVAILABLE — $60 PER WEEK

Nice room in pleasant family house
Meals and laundry included
Suits clean, tidy, quiet student

Please write to: Mrs. Elizabeth Pennykettle, 42 Wayward Crescent, Scrubbley, MA

P.S. Must like children and cats and dragons...

Sixty dollars a week. That's more like it. But wait a moment, you have to *write*? You do have some writing things in your bag, but you don't have time to mail a letter, catch a train home, and wait for a reply. But the Universe hasn't brought you this far for nothing. Already, an idea is brewing in your mind.

You go to the newsstand and ask for directions. Wayward Crescent, the man says, is about a mile away, just off the main Scrubbley road. Turn right, after Calhoun's General Store. Fifteen minutes, at a brisk walk.

Smiling, you open your bag. You find a bench and spread a writing pad over your knee.

4 Thoushall Road
Blackburn, MA

Mrs. Elizabeth Pennykettle
42 Wayward Crescent
Scrubbley, Massachusetts

Dear Mrs. Pennykettle,

Help! I am desperately in need of somewhere to stay. Next week, I am due to start a Geography course at Scrubbley College, and I haven't been able to find any housing.

I am scrupulously clean and as tidy as anyone of my age (20) can be. My hobby is reading, which is generally pretty quiet. I get along very well with children, and I love cats.

Yours sincerely,

David Rain

Mr. David Rain

P.S. I'm afraid I haven't seen any dragons around lately. I hope this isn't a problem.

That last part. The bit about dragons. That was weird. Better dragons than spiders, though. Or mice. Or eggplants.

You're wasting time. Away you go. At a brisk pace. Brisker than brisk. You're out of breath by the time you reach Calhoun's, but this is partly due to excitement now.

The Crescent is quiet. A sleepy little backwater, lined with mature trees. The sound of birds and lawn mowers is in the air. Number 42 is close to one end. It's perfect. The ideal suburban residence. Bit of a hike from Scrubbley College, but let's face it, you need the exercise.

You tiptoe down the driveway, up to the door. You push your letter through the slot, making sure the flap rattles. Then you step aside quickly so you can't be seen.

"I'll get it," cries a woman's voice.

Mrs. Pennykettle, presumably. You knock your fists together. They're home. Success!

There's a pause. You hear the sound of ripping. She's opening the envelope, reading the letter now. How long would it take? Thirty seconds? Forty? You give it fifty, with elephants in between. Then you present yourself at the door. You take a deep breath and aim your finger at the bell . . . and almost poke your would-be landlady in the eye.

Because she's opened the door already.

"Oh," you say. That wasn't supposed to happen.

She looks at you carefully, but before she speaks she glances at a small green dragon sculpture that's sitting on a shelf just inside the door. "Mmm," she says, as if the dragon might have whispered something important. Then she relaxes and says, "Hello, David."

"Erm, hello," you mutter. You want to blink, but it's hard to take your eyes off this amazing woman. She's not classically beautiful, but she is stunning. Piercing green eyes and a mane of red hair, as if plucked from at least three lions. She doesn't seem at all fazed by what you've done. But how did she know to open the door?

"Would you like to come in?"

"It's about the room," you say, rather awkwardly. You feel that you ought to explain yourself, at least.

She smiles and says, "I know. I got your letter." She waggles it and once again looks at the dragon.

Is that thing *frowning*, you wonder?

"Please," she says, opening the door a little wider. So you step into the hall. And the first thing you notice are the dragons in the window recess, halfway up the stairs. There's another one peeking through the banister rails. And another on the potted fern you've just brushed past. Little clay sculptures. All over the place. And all of them are looking at you.

Behind you, the front door closes softly. And you may think this is where the journey ends, but the truth is it's really only just beginning. An incredible journey of love and legends, adventure and magick. In a voice like a wind from another world, Mrs. Pennykettle says from behind your back, "Welcome to Wayward Crescent, David. We've been expecting you. . . ."

Chris d'Lacey, Autumn 2012

1. THE DAWN OF DRAGONS

THE EXISTENCE OF DRAGONS

Chris recently found an article on the Internet stating that if you compared the history of Earth with a calendar year, then the first cell of anything that could be called "life" did not appear until midsummer. Plants followed in August, then the various animals in the next few months. Dinosaurs arrived at the winter solstice, around December 21, and died out by the day after Christmas, the 26. Humans didn't appear until early evening of the 31, and true civilization not until four minutes to midnight. Allegedly, many living species became extinct "daily" — *Including dragons*, he thought, in a blinding flash of inspiration.

Now, I don't know about you, but to him that is a very exciting concept. Not that dragons died out, of course, but that they might actually have existed in the first place on this wonderful blue planet of ours. Imagine seeing a group of them (a flock? a wing? a *flame?*) soaring and swooping overhead in the warmth of the sun. Or beating their huge majestic wings against a fierce Arctic gale. Would you be scared silly or would you be exhilarated? Would you rush outside to stare in wonder at the spectacle, or would you cower indoors, too terrified to even peek through the window? Or would you be so used to seeing them around that you would just accept their presence and go about your normal day without paying them much attention? These are some of the questions that Chris wanted to find his own answers to when he wrote the Last Dragon Chronicles.

He is often asked whether he believes that dragons did exist on this world, and he usually replies, "I'd like to." He is in very good company. From doing some background reading, I found that while relatively few people do believe in their one-time existence, a large majority, just like Chris, would like to. What can it be about dragons that fires (sorry!) the imagination so strongly? Especially since, overall, they have had pretty lousy press.

Think of most dragon legends and myths; it seems like nine times out of ten they feature dragons as the bad guys — fire-breathing monsters who would have you for dinner as soon as look at you. Personally, I reckon all this was a ploy to keep knights in shining armor in work. What else could they do, after all, apart from rescue helpless damsels in distress? No damsels, no job. To be fair, there are some cultures around the world that do revere dragons and think them admirable creatures, *and* definitely believe that they were real. China is the most notable example, Vietnam another, and, much closer to Chris's home, Wales has its own red dragon.

But love them or loathe them, they do seem to pop up in so many countries' legends that you have to think that there is something in it. "No smoke without fire" comes to mind — a highly appropriate phrase, in the circumstances.

Perhaps there is a common folk memory or group recall from way back, or maybe it is all simply wishful thinking, that we feel that there somehow just "ought" to be dragons, to fulfill some unacknowledged and unconscious need in us all. Or, to stretch the imagination a little further, could it be that they did (still do?) exist, but on some other world, and that there was a bleed-through or crossover to this one in the dim and distant past, mentally and emotionally, if not physically? Whichever way, belief in dragons does seem to be "hardwired into the human consciousness." I don't know who came up with that phrase, but I think it sums it all up beautifully.

CHRIS D'LACEY'S DRAGONS

Although there is this huge fascination with dragons, Chris himself, when asked, always used to say that he wasn't particularly smitten with them in his early years;

he never gave them much thought. However, on closer questioning for this book, I discovered that one of his all-time favorite books from childhood is *The Hobbit*, by J. R. R. Tolkien. And guess who one of the main characters is? Smaug, a classic "bad" dragon who sits on his pile of stolen treasure and roars vengeance on anyone who dares to intrude upon him. The edition that we have even has Smaug defending his ill-gotten gains on the cover. A subtle influence there, perhaps, after all.

Chris's current take on dragons is that they are noble beasts, worthy of respect and awe, spiritual guardians of the planet and servants and defenders of Gaia, Mother Earth. But Chris does not limit himself to one type of dragon; in the Last Dragon Chronicles, there are two very different sorts — one large, one small; both benevolent. The first, as you might expect, are the *relatively* traditional "real" dragons; full-sized, immensely powerful, fire-breathing, and truly awesome. But they are birthed from eggs by parthenogenesis. . . .

The second type is more unusual still. They are about eight to ten inches tall and made from clay by one of the main characters, a potter named Elizabeth Pennykettle. She sometimes uses something called "ice-fire" in the process, which makes them into "special" dragons, that is, those that can come alive. All the dragons speak variants of a language called dragontongue, as do Liz and her daughter, Lucy, as well as the odd polar bear or two. (Yes, that's right, polar bears. I'll come to those a bit later.) These small dragons are to be found all around the Pennykettles' home, from the entrance hall to the Dragons' Den, where they are created.

David Rain, the hero of the series, even uses the Pennykettles' bathroom, which has a small "puffler" dragon named Gloria sitting on the toilet tank in front of him. She's there to "puffle" a pleasant rose scent when necessary. David does have the grace to turn her to face the wall — but whether to spare her blushes or his own, who can say?

Each of the special clay dragons that Liz creates has a particular talent or ability. There is a wishing dragon, a guard dragon (who is rather young and inexperienced and therefore always needing to check his manual for the correct procedure), a natural healing dragon, and many more. But the one you most need to know about is Gadzooks. Zookie, as he is also known, is made especially for David as a housewarming gift when he comes to lodge in the Pennykettle household, and he is an inspirational writing dragon. Gadzooks helps David get unstuck when faced with any problem — particularly writer's block. This is just as well, as David, like Chris, eventually becomes a writer. . . .

ears: can reach the size of large rose petals in a listening dragon

top knot: a sign of dragonliness

eyes: violet when active, green when solid and fooling humans

eye ridges: often raised in confusion . . .

"trumpet-shaped" nostrils: excellent for blowing smoke rings

paws: more nimble than they look, largest in a wishing dragon (like this one) →

stiff, zigzagging scales down the spine: where dragons like to be tickled . . .

scales: normally green and layered like roof slates, but can vary a lot

big flat feet: evolved after years of "stomping about"

the tail: the final arrow-shaped scale is called an "isoscele," which is thought to possess magical powers

The anatomy of a Pennykettle dragon

2. FROM SMALL ACORNS . . .

LONDON BOUND

Chris had just finished college and was working in his dad's pub, the White Horse, while sorting out what he wanted to do with his life when a friend persuaded him to move to London. The friend promised to find Chris somewhere to live and, taking up the offer, Chris soon found himself on a fast train down to the capital, followed by a slower one out to the suburbs, and ultimately knocking on the door of his new landlady in Bromley, Kent. Not at all unlike David Rain, in fact, although there were no "children, cats, or dragons" involved in Chris's case. He settled in quite readily and got on well with the family with whom he was lodging.

Making new friends, though, he thought would be quite tricky, as he was still unemployed. He regularly went into the center of the town, usually on foot due to a lack of money and a desire to get to know the area, which was entirely new to him. The outskirts of Bromley are quite leafy, but the town itself much less so, with one notable exception: the Churchill Library Gardens. Chris discovered the library quite early on — one of his favorite things to do was to take a book out and wander through the public gardens alongside until he found a sunny spot, whereupon he would sit on a wall next to a path overlooking a large stand of trees. Once settled, book in one hand, sandwich in the other, he would while away the day until it was time to go back to his digs.

One day, as he was doing exactly that, a squirrel suddenly turned up on the path nearby. It sat up on its hind legs, twitched its nose and tail (which Chris took to mean "Anything for me, please?"), and waited patiently. Being a generous sort of guy, but having only a small corner of sandwich left, he offered the squirrel that. The squirrel took it with great glee, twiddled it around in its paws a few times, and popped it into its mouth. Yum. But no — categorically not "yum" *at all* — as fast as the sandwich went in, out it came again. It was at this point that Chris discovered that squirrels can look totally disgusted. Off it went, shaking its head and spitting *puh, puh, puhhh*, every few steps. Rather taken aback by this vehement display of ingratitude, Chris was forced to the conclusion that squirrels are not terribly eager for cheese and pickle sandwiches.

Thinking no more of the incident, he shrugged his shoulders and turned his attention back to his book. Eventually, this being October, it got a little chilly. Home time. Chris mostly took the same route back to his home — it was the shortest and therefore the quickest way — but for whatever reason, on this day he found himself veering from the usual path and taking one in a slightly different direction. Such a small deviation, such a tiny decision, and yet, unbeknown to Chris, the wheels of the Universe had turned and a step was taken toward his destiny.

This new way happened to take Chris past a large oak tree. It had shed its abundant crop of acorns all over the sidewalk and far into the road. Chris was unaware of this until a car, coming too fast around the bend, sprayed him like a pellet gun with the acorns that had caught under its tires. Jolted out of his reverie, the bright idea suddenly came to him. *This is what squirrels like to eat. Acorns, not cheese and pickle sandwiches . . .*

ACORNS

The next day, he returned to the spot under the oak and gathered up every acorn he could find. Then, laden with two large brown paper bags full of squirrel delight, he retraced his steps to the library gardens and settled down in the same place as the day before. He didn't have long to wait. Within minutes, the same squirrel appeared on the path by his side. Chris was sure of it. Perhaps it was just the play of shadows on its face in the autumn sunshine, but it definitely seemed to *wink* at him in a knowing way. Slightly disturbed by this, but determined to make up for his sandwich mistake, he tentatively offered up an acorn. The squirrel took one open-eyed look, made a fast grab for it, and guzzled it on the spot. Success!

The squirrel thought so, too. It sat wide-eyed and waiting. Chris obliged with another nut. This time the creature twitched it in its paws as before, but then ran across the pathway and between some railings, burying the acorn in the loose soil to be found there. That done, it immediately came back for "thirds." Once more Chris obliged. The squirrel ran up a nearby tree and deposited the acorn somewhere within a hole in one of the branches, promptly returning for another go, obviously thinking all its Christmases must have come at once. However, when it reached Chris this time, a second squirrel was being fed a nut. Then a third, a fourth, a fifth arrived . . . until within a very short space of time there were no less than seventeen squirrels all feasting and scrabbling around Chris's feet. Some of the tamer ones even plucked up enough courage to run up his legs and perch on his lap, the bravest of all sticking its furry little head right into his coat pocket. He'd certainly made a lot of new friends — and much quicker than he'd expected!

At this point a woman pushing a baby buggy came along the path, holding the hand of a young girl of four or five. They stopped to watch the scene before them. The young girl pointed and in a piping little voice said, "Ooh, look, Mummy. It's the squiwwel man." And so it turned out to be, but many more years were to pass before the world at large became aware of that fact.

THE START OF SOMETHING . . .

Ten years later, Chris was working as a lab technician at Leicester University Medical School and, being an enthusiastic songwriter, was writing and recording in his spare time. However, with full-time employment, there wasn't much of that available. Looking to find a less energy-intensive way of expressing his creativity, he decided to drop the music temporarily and focus on just the words. *Writing*, he thought. *How difficult can that be?* Ha! Famous last words, almost. His office wastebasket (and the surrounding area) quickly filled up with scrunched-up bits of paper. Failed attempts at a science fiction short story. Failed attempts at short, long, middling, *any* kinds of story. Frustration reigned. But Chris is nothing if not persistent. He decided as a final try to write a cutesy little tale as a Christmas present for me. Romantic soul, eh?

For a previous Christmas present, Chris had bought me a polar bear stuffed animal, which he'd put outside in the backyard, leaving him with one paw raised against the back door, as if he were knocking. Chris's story was to be something very simple: how Boley the polar bear had arrived in our backyard from the North Pole. Easy.

Christmas present extraordinaire

But no, not easy. Chris had barely gotten two paragraphs written when he realized that he knew nothing about polar bears except that they are white and live at the North Pole. Wrong on both counts, actually — their hair is hollow, and is more of a cream color because of it; and they live right across the Arctic ice cap — *except* at the Pole. Oh, well. A trip to the local library was called for. Mission achieved, Chris returned home with a book called *The World of the Polar Bear*, by Thor Larsen, intending to cherry-pick a few interesting snippets to dot around the cutesy little tale. He began writing. And writing. And writing. The tale took

two and a half years to complete. All *250,000 words*
of it. Six hundred pages; longhand.

I remember this very well; I typed it.

This *little tale*, if nothing else, taught Chris the craft
of writing. It was ultimately named *White Fire*, and
parts of it were used in the dragon books, as if written
by David Rain, who also writes a book called *White
Fire*. It should be stressed, however, that the two books
are not the same. David's is an ecological plea to save
polar bears and the planet; Chris's goes much further
than that, being a grand saga involving the Inuit people,
white men (researchers, hunters, etc.) from the south,
and great dynasties of polar bears. It has never seen the
light of day and remains dormant in a desk drawer,
awaiting — who knows what?

"White fire" is a metaphor for spirituality, and this
first book sowed the seed for the dragon books. It
was written partly at home, early mornings and late
evenings, and partly during Chris's tea breaks at the
university. It was written longhand because (believe it
or not) this was still in an age when computers were

few and far between. Chris's whole department at the university had only one, for instance. He eventually "graduated" to using this machine, but until that time, his trusty pen and pad were his tools of the trade. It became a standing joke among his colleagues that Chris wouldn't be going to the break room with them, he would be "writing his bestselling novel, ha-ha."

One day, one such colleague walked into the room where the computer was housed and said, "Still writing about polar bears? Can't you write about anything else?"

Chris stopped, left a blank line, and began, "It was a beautiful autumn morning in the library gardens . . ."

To this day, he does not know why he did this — or where it came from. He refers to it as his "Tolkien moment." (Apparently J. R. R. Tolkien, a professor at the time he wrote *The Hobbit*, and grading exam papers, came upon a blank sheet of paper within the pile. It is alleged that he, for no apparent reason, wrote: "In a hole in the ground there lived a hobbit." Of such moments careers are made.)

SQUIRRELS

"What's that about?" chimed said colleague.

"I think it's about squirrels," Chris replied, mystified.

Exit colleague, guffawing to all within earshot, "You won't believe this! He's writing about squirrels now!" Gales of laughter ensued.

By then, however, Chris was beginning to appreciate the importance of such inspirational moments and he followed up the idea. The story poured out in a phenomenal rush. He decided to take a break from *White Fire* when he realized that, at this speed, he could probably write the squirrel story as my Christmas present instead as, clearly, the polar bear one would not be finished in time.

Knowing nothing about this intended gift I snoozed on unawares while Chris got up extra early in the mornings, trogged across the local park to the university, wrote another chapter of the book, returned home, brought me a cup of tea (still with his outdoor coat on — I assumed he was just off to the lab, rather than returning from it), had breakfast, and then went back to work for the normal start of the day. Bless him, he kept this up for over two months. And I got my story.

The inspiration for its setting was the Churchill Library Gardens in Bromley. Chris had always retrospectively felt guilty for gathering up all the acorns by the roadside on his way home that far-off day, as he later realized that although he had been helping the squirrels in the gardens, he had almost certainly also

The library gardens, Scrubbley — or should that be Bromley?

been depriving those around the tree of their own "harvest." He therefore wrote the story line the reverse way around — the acorns were stolen *from* the library gardens to be "donated" elsewhere, in fact to trap and subsequently aid an injured squirrel named Conker. Quite an ethical guy, then, after all.

The story (entitled *The Adventures of Snigger the Squirrel*) begins with Snigger and the rest of the library gardens' squirrels waking up one morning expecting to find a huge nutfall, as it has been very windy the night before. However, upon reaching the clearing where the abundance of acorns should have been, it is obvious that something terrible has happened because there is not a sign of a single nut anywhere. . . .

"But where are they all?" said Snigger, astonished to find that the ground was not carpeted with the fruit of the tree, as in previous years.

A female squirrel, Cherrylea, replied, "There was a nutfall. There was. I saw it. . . . Last night, the eve of nutfall, I lay tossing and turning in my drey, too excited by the prospect of the forthcoming harvest to sleep. I'm sure many of you were the same way." Several heads nodded in support. Cherrylea continued: "As you know, my drey overlooks the clearing. For much of the night I could hear the wind whistling through the branches, wrapping itself around them and shaking the acorns clear. Down they came like raindrops on the pond, plopping into the leaf-fall below in such numbers that I was tempted to leave the drey right then and begin the harvest by the beam of the lamplight that shines through the dark hours.... But knowing that would be unfair to those of you who drey over the hill, I resisted all such temptation."

Cherrylea swallowed hard, her mouth dry with fear, her tail twitching nervously. "I did leave my drey last night," she began, "but I only went as far as the old stump tree," she added loudly, referring to a large sycamore that had had several branches sawn in half some years before to prevent them crashing through the windows of the library building. "I was so excited. I knew there would be nuts everywhere. Everywhere!" she *said, opening out her short front legs and doing a little turn to indicate the extent of the fall. "I was about to run back to my drey when suddenly a great dark shadow spread all across the ground where we are now standing." The squirrels looked nervously about them, some moved closer to their friends. "I was very fright- ened. . . . The last thing I remember before fleeing to my drey was seeing a horrid black beast scuffling about among the leaves . . . collecting up our nutfall."*

The "horrid black beast," or rather *nutbeast*, that Cherrylea refers to is, of course, a man, dressed in a long black coat . . . and this is the first appearance of the character who, much later, became David Rain, the hero of the Last Dragon Chronicles.

3. . . . To Grand Dragons

WRITING FOR CHILDREN

Over the next few years, Chris finished *White Fire*, and then found he could turn his hand to other genres and other lengths of story at will. He wrote short stories for adults and had some reasonable success, being published regularly in small-press magazines, and receiving excellent feedback from the writing competitions he entered, but few prizes.

One day, a friend at the local writers' group that he attended (and still does, nearly thirty years on) gave him a leaflet for a competition to write for children. It was to be a story of 3,000 words, the prize was £2,000 (just over $3,000 US dollars), and the winner and eleven runners-up were to be published in an anthology. Up to this point, Chris had not tried his hand at writing for children at all. He thought he would give it a go. How hard could it be? Very, is the answer to that one. Very, very, very.

He was back to crumpling paper in frustration, though that was more difficult to do now that he had progressed to using a computer and printer (thus several rain forests' worth of paper were saved in the d'Lacey household by the advent of modern technology). He continued to struggle with writing (or rather, *not* writing) this story. He hemmed, he hawed, he pondered, he wailed. The deadline was looming; up popped an idea.

He had a story called *Ice*, written for adults, with an environmental theme: the hole in the ozone layer, which was very current at that time. But Chris had never been able to sell it. If he changed it around so that it was told through the eyes of a child, maybe it would work. . . .

He rewrote the story. He entered the competition. He didn't win. Or get into the anthology. *Ah well, that's me done with kids' stuff,* he thought, but he read it aloud to his writer friends and one of them suggested he send it to a publisher. He did some research and sent off his manuscript. A while later he received a phone call from a lovely lady saying she would like to buy his story. Knowing no better, he was very pleased, but that's all. If Chris had known then how incredibly difficult it is to get picked up off what is called the "slush pile" (that is the pile of unsolicited manuscripts sent in by hopeful would-be authors), he might have just decided to stay in bed. Or juggle with his socks.

Nevertheless, at thirty-nine-and-three-quarters years old, Chris became a published children's author with *A Hole at the Pole,* as it was subsequently named. One book does not a children's author make. However, on the strength of it, Chris managed to get a literary agent, and further children's books were written — and published. They were all for quite young children, but his agent suggested that he attempt a longer work, a novel, for a slightly older age group.

Chris suggested she look at *Snigger.* But "talking

animal" books were not in vogue, so that got a thumbs-down. Could he rework it? Turn it around so it was told from the viewpoint of humans? Would that help? Perhaps a character, let's call him David, could come to lodge with a mom-and-daughter single-parent family? The daughter would be squirrel-crazy and want him to help her save an injured one that was running around in the yard. David would be the "nutbeast" who "steals" the nutfall to attempt to catch — Conker, of course. The rewrite took place. Eventually Chris plucked up enough courage to show his editor the revised squirrel story, now renamed *Snigger and the Nutbeast.* Overall, she liked the story, but felt it was lacking in certain areas. Among many very good suggestions she offered was that of giving the mother in the story a job. Chris agreed, but was at a loss as to what Mrs. Pennykettle could do. He knew that he wanted it to be somewhat artistic or creative, and done from home. Nothing suggested itself, but there was no rush. The Universe would provide in its own good time.

THE ARRIVAL OF GADZOOKS

The answer came from a cheery lady named Val Chivers. Val, along with her husband, Peter, has become a dear friend over the years, but we didn't know that on that chilly weekend so long ago. Chris and I had a rare day off, and we decided to go to a local craft fair at a place called Stoughton Farm Park. There were the usual stalls — lavender cushions, wheat bags, jewelry, wooden toys. And then there were dragons. Val's fabulous and wonderfully inventive clay dragons. They were green, mostly, a few bluer than green. Eight to ten inches tall, *gorgeous*. We couldn't take our eyes off them. But in those days we were broke most of the time, and although the dragons weren't expensive, we couldn't possibly afford one.

Val saw us looking longingly and started up a conversation during which we explained our plight. Perhaps she could put one aside for us until we could get enough money together to buy it? Instead, Val pointed us toward a corner of the stall we hadn't noticed: CASUALTY CORNER.

*Val Chivers creating her amazing
dragons*

Here were dragons with slight imperfections — missing toes, chipped spines, streaky glaze. Each for the price of five pounds (about eight US dollars). *That* we could afford.

I raised my head in delight, only to lock eyes with the dragon we just knew was ours. We paid for him and said a happy good-bye to Val, never thinking that we would see her again. In the car on the way back home I held our new companion in my lap. Having been chatting about our day, we were stopped at a traffic light, when Chris suddenly yelled out, "She's a potter! Elizabeth Pennykettle is a potter, and she makes clay dragons, which she sells at the local market. And she has them dotted all around the house as ornaments." The small clay dragon twitched his tail on my knee, I swear it.

This minor revelation, among many other changes, was written into *Snigger* and duly sent back to Chris's editor for her approval. She definitely saw the potential in the story, but had one more comment to make: "Can we do something more with the dragons?" she said, quite innocently. *"Can they come to life?"*

Chris began the mammoth task of a wholesale rewrite once more. It took months. But eventually the dragons were woven in throughout the whole manuscript. Once the concept of "living" dragons was accepted, they did indeed seem to have lives — and abilities — of their own. It helped that we remembered that Val had created different characters for her clay dragons. Ones with large ears: in Chris's mind they became listening dragons. One with a bunch of flowers became a potions dragon, able to influence people by getting them to sniff her bouquet. Another had overlarge paws — it now became a wishing dragon, and so on. Other characters, created by us, have then inspired Val to create further varieties of dragons. Thus she has made Gollygosh Golightly, for instance, who carries a magical toolbox. (More of him later, in the "Who's Who" chapter.)

However, the most relevant dragon, the one we purchased initially and named Gadzooks (the best fiver we have *ever* spent), turned out to be the key to retaining the squirrels in the story in a very natural way. As we perceived him, he had a notepad and pencil in his paws — an inspirational writing dragon, obviously. So Chris had David write a story, within Chris's own story, for Lucy Pennykettle's eleventh birthday present, Gadzooks helping him when he gets stuck. David reads parts of it to Lucy throughout the latter part of Chris's book. Success at last! It was to be published.

JUST THE BEGINNING

Book covers are generally thought out and produced long before the book itself is published, or even finished sometimes. Because Chris's book was originally conceived as a squirrel book, and also went through various changes of style, content, and approach, before settling on the dragon element as dominant, it was a long and tricky job to get the covers right. The accompanying illustrations demonstrate what I mean. They are just a selection of roughs that were suggested, mulled over, and eventually rejected as being unsuitable for one reason or another.

Early attempts at covers

A different approach . . .

Various ideas were tossed about until someone at the publisher came up with the genius idea of using a dragon's eye on the cover. A very rough illustration of this was produced and approved as a concept, and then an artist was hired to do justice to the suggested idea. The artist concerned did more than that. He created an exceptional and iconic cover painting — which became the precursor for the whole of the series. That phenomenally talented artist is named Angelo Rinaldi. He very generously contributed the following information about his work for the books.

"*Regarding the first cover, I was closely art-directed and given a fairly detailed brief to produce a close-up of a pottery dragon's eye. This was before I had the luxury of the Internet to do any referencing, so I went hunting in old bric-a-brac shops and found some green*

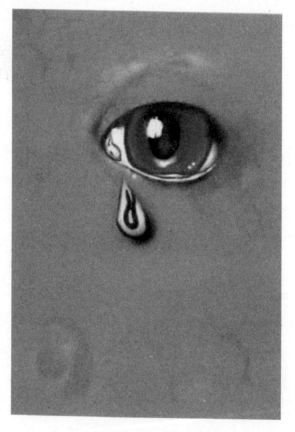

A breakthrough idea at last

An unused rough for Dark Fire

china figurines. I then took some inspiration from Chinese dragons and worked up a pencil drawing, which went through a few minor corrections regarding the shape of the eye and the teardrop. And then it was on to artwork, which is oil painted on canvas board to give the cover a distinctive textured look. The main challenge with the first set of covers in the series was making the dragon look like it was made of pottery, and alive! Of course by the time I came to do the later ones, I had the Internet at my disposal for referencing. For example, The Fire Eternal benefited from some great reference of a Chinese golden dragon. The last piece of artwork for Rain and Fire was a departure from the series style, in that it was more illustrative and less design-led. I did several pencil sketches for this cover; in some the dragon looked more reptilian, in others too human, but I think we reached the right balance in the final piece."

Over the rewrite period it also became obvious that a change of title was required. *Snigger and the Nutbeast* was hardly the right title for a dragon book. A total rethink was called for. Although several titles were passed around for consideration, it was always Chris's intention to have the "new" book called *The Fire Within*. For him, "the fire within" represents the creative spark and, with the creation of Gadzooks as an externalized version of that, clearly that was what the book was all about.

Chris was doing a school visit one day, and was explaining that *The Fire Within* was a metaphor. Having established that the children knew what a metaphor was, he brightly asked if anyone would like to have a guess at "A metaphor for what?" There was a pause. Silence. Then one brave lad put his hand up and said, rather hesitantly, "Is it heartburn?" Chris no longer asks that question in his talks.

The Fire Within was finally published in the United Kingdom in 2000. It did very well (and still does — it's past its twenty-fifth reprint), and was long-listed for the Carnegie Medal. It was then published in the United States in 2005. Reader response was very positive and Chris felt that he could write more on the subject — but even he had no idea that there would be so much story

to tell, and that it would eventually take seven books —
the Last Dragon Chronicles — to do it.

REAL DRAGONS

By this time, Chris was getting fan mail from all over
the world via his Web site. Over a hundred e-mails a
week were arriving, from adults and children alike, all
greatly enthusiastic about the Pennykettle dragons, but
many also wanting to know if (a) there was going to
be another book, and (b) if so, could it have "real" (i.e.
large, fire-breathing) dragons in it, as well, please.
Interesting. "As well," not "instead of."

Happy to oblige, off Chris went to do some research
about big dragons. At the library, he was ushered over
to a bookshelf crammed to the ceiling with book upon
book about dragons.

"All these?" Chris whimpered.

"And these. And those. And the ones over there,"
responded the librarian. Chris collapsed in a small
heap (quite difficult when you're six foot two). Having

been assisted back to his feet, he shambled out of the library and wandered off down the street, practically gibbering.

After that experience, he decided to simply make it all up. Thus a lady at one of his book-signing events, upon asking him how much research he did ("It must have taken you *years*. . . ."), was rather taken aback when Chris said, "None," and then promptly ran away to hide in the bathroom. It all seems to have worked out for the best, though — check out chapter 7 on "Myths and Legends" to see if you agree.

The second book in the series, *Icefire*, was published in the UK two years later (in 2006 in the US), and yes, the series does contain big dragons from there onward. Following the dragon-eye cover concept, Angelo Rinaldi this time painted an ice blue illustration, with an Arctic landscape reflected within the pupil of the dragon's eye. By the time the third book, *Fire Star*, came out (red, with a fire star within the eye), Chris's books were becoming a definite "brand," being called the Fire series or Dragon series by the fans, and even sometimes by the publishers. The fourth book, *The Fire Eternal*, was published next (gold cover, the Earth in the eye), followed by *Dark Fire*, which has a very dark blue, almost black, cover, and a darkling (or "antidragon") in the eye.

It was at this point that the publishers wanted a "proper" title for the series, and it officially became the Last Dragon Chronicles. And in fact, *Dark Fire* has the series title mentioned within its pages as part of the story line. Book six, *Fire World*, has an orange cover. The eye contains an image of a firebird, a brand-new creature featured in the story. It's somewhere between a bird and a dragon. The final book, called *The Fire Ascending*, is a brilliant blue-purple color and features a young girl with wings within the eye.

Initially, it seemed to be quite a task to find a definitive title for the series. It wasn't until Chris stopped and thought, *Whose story is this, really?* that it became apparent that it was not actually David Rain's, but Gawain's — the last known "big" dragon in the world. Once that was established, it was simple.

4. WHO'S WHO: THE CHARACTERS

There are over a hundred and fifty named characters in the Last Dragon Chronicles. Human beings, squirrels, and the little clay dragons made by Elizabeth Pennykettle dominate the first book in the series, *The Fire Within*. From there on the character base broadens out substantially and we meet polar bears, "natural" dragons, firebirds, unicorns, alien life-forms (both "good" and "evil"), and even Mother Earth. The following list focuses on those characters who play major roles in the series, even though some of them may appear only briefly, or in a single book.

THE HUMANS — EARTH

DAVID RAIN: The hero of the books. He first appears as a young college student, when he becomes a tenant of the Pennykettle family. His curiosity about the clay dragons that Elizabeth (Liz) Pennykettle makes drives the whole series and fuels his increasingly dangerous investigations into the existence, history, and mythology of dragons. As his journey progresses, we learn that there is a lot more to David than the innocent young man he first appears to be. In *Dark Fire* it is revealed that his connection to dragons runs very deep, and that his mission of discovery has been preplanned by a greater intelligence called the Fain in an effort to prepare the Earth, and the human race, for a new era of dragon colonization. This brings him into conflict with many enemies, principally the sibyl, Gwilanna. By the final book of the series, he even has to travel through time in his attempts to defeat her and to fulfill his destiny.

ELIZABETH (LIZ) PENNYKETTLE: The mother of Lucy Pennykettle, Liz lives at 42 Wayward Crescent in Scrubbley. Liz is a potter with a difference. She has the ability to make clay dragons that she can bring to life. Among the many dragons she makes in the series, the most important is probably Gadzooks, whom she makes as a housewarming gift for David. Liz is a distant but direct descendant of Guinevere, a woman who was with Gawain, the last known natural dragon in the world, when he died. Naturally, Liz has inherited her own "dragon-ness" from Guinevere.

LUCY PENNYKETTLE: The feisty daughter of Liz Pennykettle. Lucy is just short of her eleventh birthday when David first comes into her life. She is sixteen by the time of the events of *The Fire Ascending*. She regards David as something of the "big brother" that she never had. Her initial insistence that he help her save an injured squirrel leads to the discovery of David's ability to write stories (with the aid of Gadzooks). The books that David writes for Lucy (particularly a polar bear saga called *White Fire*) help to establish David as a cult author and indirectly draw Lucy into an edgy friendship with journalist Tam Farrell.

SUZANNA (ZANNA) MARTINDALE: The longterm girlfriend of David and later the mother of his daughter, Alexa. Zanna and David meet in *Icefire* when she is a sparky Goth student. Her knowledge of all things New Age aids his investigations into dragon lore. Ultimately, it is revealed that Zanna is a sibyl, able to perform certain kinds of magicks. Although she loves David deeply, their relationship is often rocky and they clash frequently over Alexa's upbringing. After many twists and turns, they resolve their differences and have a happy life together.

ARTHUR MERRIMAN: A brilliant physicist who is continually wrangling with the mysteries of the Universe and the power of human consciousness and creativity. He first meets Liz when he is a postgraduate student living in Cambridge, Massachusetts, and falls in love with her. Their relationship is temporarily broken off when the sibyl Gwilanna tricks him into believing that Liz's love for him is not genuine. Distraught, Arthur joins a monastery and adopts the name Brother Vincent. At the monastery, he finds a claw of Gawain and is empowered to write about David, little knowing that he is manipulating the so-called dark matter of the Universe to create David's character. In *Fire Star*, he is reunited with Liz and thereafter lives with the family at Wayward Crescent.

GWILANNA: More of a nuisance than an out-and-out villain, Gwilanna is a sibyl and a kind of specialized midwife who, like Guinevere, was around when the dragon Gawain died. Unlike Guinevere, Gwilanna has survived for thousands of years, keeping herself alive by the clever use of elixirs brewed from one of Gawain's scales. Arrogantly regarding herself as superior to any human, she constantly clashes with David. What saves her from his wrath on more than one occasion is her ancient knowledge of dragons and her role in the development of the descendants of Guinevere, e.g., Liz and Lucy Pennykettle.

ANDERS BERGSTROM: A mysterious and extremely influential character who first appears in *Icefire* as David's college tutor. He guides David in his investigations, teaching him about the connection between dragons and polar bears. Over the course of the series it transpires that Bergstrom was a polar scientist who vanished, in mysterious circumstances, on an Arctic exploration to the remote Hella glacier. Thought to have been killed by a polar bear, Bergstrom has actually harmonized his life force with Thoran, the first polar bear ever to walk the Arctic ice. Bergstrom, in his role as an ambassador for raising awareness about the Arctic (particularly the dangers of global warming), was responsible for giving the young Liz Pennykettle (as a child) a snowball containing dragon auma, which she, now an adult, uses to animate her clay dragons.

HENRY BACON: A librarian who lives at 41 Wayward Crescent and a longtime, well-meaning but grumpy next-door neighbor to the Pennykettles. Although always on the periphery of the stories, Henry's significance grows when it is discovered that his grandfather was in the same party of explorers as Anders Bergstrom. In *Dark Fire*, Henry's collection of memorabilia connected with his grandfather's explorations provides direct evidence of the ancient existence of dragons.

TAM FARRELL: A journalist who first comes to prominence in *The Fire Eternal* when he tries to uncover the truth about David's background. His attempts to use Zanna to get information on David almost results in her killing him with magicks. He makes amends when he twice rescues Lucy from the malevolent thought-beings, the Ix (an offshoot of the Fain), and thereafter becomes an ally of the family.

ALEXA MARTINDALE: See also **Agawin**. Arguably the most important character in the whole series. Alexa is the charming daughter of David and Zanna. Her abilities, which include telepathy with David and an apparent ability to predict the future, are largely ignored as a kind of advanced (but slightly expected) precociousness. Her importance starts to come to the forefront when she is five years old, in *Dark Fire*. In *The Fire Eternal*, to Zanna's amazement, she begins to grow wings, and as a result, is sometimes known as Angel. The literal meaning of the name "Alexa" is "protector of mankind" and she more than lives up to this role in *The Fire Ascending*.

SOPHIE PRENTICE: David's first girlfriend. She appears toward the end of the first book, collecting donations for a local wildlife hospital. She helps Lucy Pennykettle and David look after Snigger and Conker, two squirrels who feature heavily in *The Fire Within*. Conker has an eye injury caused by a crow named Caractacus.

GUINEVERE: A young woman from the mists of time who held a passionate desire to see dragons survive.

Although she is mostly mentioned as a character of legend, Guinevere's role in the story is hugely important, for she was present when the last-known natural dragon, Gawain, died. She caught Gawain's fire tear, setting off a chain of events that is still continuing to the present day, through her descendants Liz and Lucy Pennykettle.

AGAWIN: Begins life as a simple goatherd on early Earth, but becomes involved in an epic journey to save one of the final twelve dragons, Galen, from the clutches of the Ix-controlled Voss. Although Galen perishes, Agawin catches a spark of his fire. This has many remarkable benefits, one of which is to be physically transformed on the point of his own death and reborn as Alexa Martindale, David and Zanna's daughter. From there on in, he/she aids David in a battle to prevent Gwilanna altering the Earth's timeline and destroying everything they know and love. Agawin narrates the major part of *The Fire Ascending* and even features as a grown-up Alexa at the end of the book.

VOSS: Appears in *The Fire Ascending* as a common man who becomes infected by the Ix and is used by them to capture a unicorn and break his horn. This gives him power over men and other creatures. The Ix intend to use Voss to capture the dying dragon, Galen, so that they might invert his fire to create a darkling. This ambition is initially thwarted by Agawin, but Voss returns and raises a darkling army when his daughter, Gwilanna, attempts to change the timeline.

GRELLA: A young woman who takes care of Gwilanna as a baby, even though she is not her mother. Grella comes from the district of Taan, a region in the far north on early Earth. The Taan are well known for making tapestries, at which Grella excels. Her family befriends Agawin and they encourage him to try making a tapestry of his own. Although not skilled at drawing, Agawin produces a faithful representation of the Pennykettle dragon, Gadzooks, whom he has seen in a vision. After this, the picture seems to gain a life of its own. It grows and changes to become what is known as the *Tapestry of Isenfier*, which first appears in the librarium building in *Fire World*.

JOSEPH HENRY: The unborn son of Arthur and Liz whose spirit leaves his mother's body when the family is threatened by a spark of dark fire. Joseph enters the form of the Pennykettle dragon Gwillan and becomes heavily involved in David's quest to prevent Gwilanna malevolently altering the Earth's timeline. Toward the end of the series, it becomes apparent that Joseph has been the guiding force behind all those on the side of good.

THE HUMANS — CO:PERN:ICA

DAVID MERRIMAN: David Rain in one of his other guises.

ELIZA MERRIMAN: An alternative Elizabeth Pennykettle. "Mother" of David.

PENNY MERRIMAN: A different version of Lucy Pennykettle. "Sister" of David.

ROSA: Looks after the librarium (a museum of books) for Mr. Henry. She is the Co:pern:ican version of Zanna.

HARLAN MERRIMAN: Arthur Merriman in another probable life. "Father" of David.

AUNT GWYNETH: Known as Gwilanna, in the earlier books — but still up to her old tricks.

COUNSELOR STRØMBERG: Another version of Anders Bergstrom. He investigates the young David's disturbing dreams.

MR. CHARLES HENRY: Henry Bacon's alternative self. Curator of the librarium in Bushley, Co:pern:ica's version of Scrubbley.

MATHEW LEFARR: Tam Farrell in this world. Like Lucy with Tam on Earth, Penny has strong feelings for Mathew.

ANGEL: See **Alexa Martindale** (on Earth). Angel is capable of "Traveling" across the time nexus between worlds, in much the same way as her father, David, can.

THE CLAY DRAGONS

GADZOOKS: An inspirational writing dragon with a powerful ability to make events happen simply by writing down words on the notepad he carries. He guides David throughout the series and is influential in all the major developments of the story.

GROYNE: More birdlike than dragon and allegedly created for Anders Bergstrom by an Inuit shaman, not by Liz Pennykettle. Tremendously powerful, he can make himself invisible, morph into different shapes (particularly a small piece of narwhal tusk), and move whomever is carrying him through time and space.

GRETEL: A potions dragon who casts spells in the scents of flowers. Initially made for Gwilanna, she later defects to Zanna.

G'RETH: A dragon with the ability to grant wishes (but only if beneficial to dragonkind). He is the first point of contact with the thought-beings, the Fain.

GOLLYGOSH GOLIGHTLY: A healing dragon made by David. Golly can heal ailments but is more often employed in fixing or solving mechanical or electrical problems.

GWENDOLEN: Specifically Lucy's special dragon and a whiz at IT. She comes to Lucy's rescue on many occasions.

GWILLAN: A kind and loving "house" dragon who helps Liz with domestic duties and ultimately has a hugely significant role.

GRUFFEN: A slightly hopeless guard dragon, often involved on the periphery of dramatic events. He's very young and new to the job, so he has to keep referring to his manual for the correct procedures to follow.

GRACE: A "listening" dragon. She has the ability to pick up and beam signals from and to Liz, David, etc., or any of the other Pennykettle dragons.

GAUGE: A dragon with the unique ability to tell (and measure) time.

GLADE: Glade is a rarity — a Pennykettle dragon who lives with a "normal" family (that of Lucy's friend, Melanie). Glade can detect and predict changes in mood. She enters the story in *Dark Fire*.

GAWAIN AND GUINEVERE: Two of Liz's clay dragons who rarely leave her pottery studio, the Dragons' Den. They have been named by her in tribute to their ancient namesakes. Their role is to "kindle" other clay dragons into life. They are deeply mysterious and rarely mentioned.

THE LISTENER/GANZFELD: Although he lives in the Pennykettle household, Ganzfeld was not made by Liz. He is, however, the template for all those she *did* make. He is never referred to by name until the final stages of the series. Like Grace, he has the ability to receive and send messages. He sits atop the fridge in the kitchen at Wayward Crescent, quietly absorbing everything that goes on.

THE NATURAL DRAGONS

GAWAIN: He is the "last dragon" that the series title refers to. At the end of the last great age of dragons on the Earth, he was the final dragon to die. When he shed his fire tear (documented in *Icefire*), he left behind him a legacy which fuels the whole series.

GAWAINE: A queen dragon, mother of Gawain.

GROCKLE: A modern-day dragon born when Zanna and Liz "kindle" an egg between them. At the end of *Fire Star* he is taken by the Fain into their home world, Ki:mera, but returns to aid David in *Dark Fire*.

G'OREAL: A powerful ice dragon and the leader of the new "Wearle" (or clan) which has been sent to recolonize the Earth.

GALEN: A dragon who comes to Kasgerden, a mountainous region on old Earth, to die. He is one of the last twelve dragons and is hugely significant in Agawin's story, related in *The Fire Ascending*.

THE FIREBIRDS

GIDEON: Not actually a firebird himself, Gideon is an eagle who goes through an amazing transformation to begin the firebird line.

AURIELLE: Cream and apricot colored; she is the sweetest creature, adorable and highly intelligent. She guards the *Tapestry of Isenfier* and spends her days trying to make sense of it.

AZKIAR: Red; feisty and cross most of the time, but with a soft spot for Aurielle. He attacks David one day in the mistaken belief that David has injured another firebird, setting off a chain of events which leads to the tapestry finally being understood.

AUBREY: Sky blue; goes to investigate a ripple in the fabric of time but falls foul of the Ix, who turn him black and use him for their own devious ends.

ALERON (ALSO KNOWN AS RUNCEY): Green; the first firebird to take a specific interest in the human world. He often follows David and Rosa around the librarium and is the unfortunate victim of an accident that results in Azkiar attacking David.

THE POLAR BEARS

THORAN: Originally a brown bear, he helps the woman Guinevere to escape from Gwilanna after Gawain, the last-known natural dragon, has shed his fire tear. In an extraordinary moment of magicks, he is turned into the first white bear to walk the polar ice cap and thereafter becomes a creature of legend.

LOREL: One of nine polar bears that ruled the ice at the time of Thoran. Lorel is a Teller of Ways. His ability is to record, remember, and recount all the legends of the Arctic.

RAGNAR: A fighting bear and another ruler of the ice. He is immortalized in legend when he sheds a tooth and beats it into the ice, apparently creating an island which comes to be known as the Tooth of Ragnar, though there is some debate as to the validity of this story.

INGAVAR, AVREL, AND KAILAR: These three bears are the modern-day equivalent of Thoran, Lorel, and Ragnar. The most important of them is Ingavar, who is present when David fights a dramatic battle with an agent of the Ix at the end of *Fire Star*. The spirits of Ingavar and David merge, and David can thereafter appear in either form at will. At the end of *Dark Fire*, the ice bear population of Earth is taken away to the Fain dimension, Ki:mera, but the bears, led by Avrel and Kailar, return to engage Voss and his darklings in *The Fire Ascending*.

MISCELLANEOUS OTHERS

SNIGGER AND CONKER:

Two of many squirrels who
used to live on Wayward
Crescent. The tree where
they used to drey was cut
down, so the majority of them
moved away. Conker gets left
behind because he is injured.
Snigger returns to assist in his capture,
so that he can be examined by a wildlife vet.

CARACTACUS: A crow who
injures Conker the squirrel when
he gets too close to the crow's
nest. Conker means no harm,
but the crow is brutal in
defense of his young, who
are about to hatch.

BONNINGTON: The Pennykettles' cat. He is transformed from a lazy, slightly stupid tabby into a creature of wonder when he "commingles" with a Fain entity in

Fire Star. He rarely gets involved with the Pennykettle dragons (he knows minimal dragontongue, they even less felinespeak) but does come to their aid in times of trouble. On Co:pern:ica, Bonnington's equivalent, a katt, is called *Boon.*

WINSTON: David's teddy bear. Does not have a large role to play, but he's there or thereabouts in the background.

BRONSON: A toy mammoth belonging to Alexa. She sends a thought projection of him to

David in the Arctic at a crucial point in *The Fire Eternal*.

GAIA: The spirit of the Earth; Earth Mother. Appears in a variety of guises and semi-physical forms throughout the series. Helps Lucy, particularly in times of need. Also creates Ganzfeld, Liz's listening dragon.

THE FAIN: A mysterious race of beings who first enter the saga in *Fire Star* when G'reth, the wishing dragon, makes contact with one of them. The Fain have no physical body and exist in another dimension on a plane of thought, manipulating the dark energy of the Universe to create a thought-world known as Ki:mera around them (though this is never seen). The Fain can "commingle" with any physical life-form, but regard dragons as the most perfect form there is. The Fain's spiritual development depends upon them commingling with the "white fire" of a living dragon, a process called "illumination." They frequently come to prominence as the story progresses, but their history with the human race is checkered, largely because humans and dragons have, in the past, struggled to live in harmony together on the Earth. On the alternative world of Co:pern:ica, the Fain collectively call themselves *The Higher*.

THE IX: In effect, the flipside of the Fain. They are in a continuous unseen war with the Fain, seeking to gain control of the dark energy of the Universe to manipulate it for their own evil ends. In the past, they have attempted to use the imaginative power of humans to their advantage, leaving shadows of darkness in the human psyche (gargoyles, bogeymen, fear of spiders, etc.). Dragons are the physical enemy of the Ix, but the Ix have countered them by producing a template for an antidragon, a creature they call a darkling. Darklings are terrifying monsters, but are no match for dragons, because so far the Fain have been able to prevent the Ix from creating "dark fire," the most destructive force in the Universe, which the Ix would need if they were ever to "delumine" one of their darklings.

CHARACTER NAMES

When Chris is invited to speak in schools, one of the questions he is always asked is "Where do you get the characters' names from?" He usually replies that they just pop up when they're needed. Although this is accurate, it's worth citing a few examples of how this happens.

A good place to start would be with David Rain, since he's the hero of the series. Chris was always fascinated by the stories he was taught in religion class. He particularly enjoyed those about David (later King David) and they stood out in his memory. Thus "David" comes from the Bible.

"Rain" is from a completely different source. Chris is a huge Beatles fan and many years ago they released a double-A-sided single with the songs "Paperback Writer" and "Rain." Since Chris wanted to be the former, he thought his alter ego, David (who is based on Chris in his younger days), ought to be the latter. And while we're still on the subject of the Beatles, you might like to know that David's teddy bear is named after Chris's all-time hero, and the person Chris would most like to have met, John Lennon. Winston was John's middle name.

The Pennykettle last name is based on a previous neighbor of Chris's. As a boy he used to live next door to a family with the last name Kettle. Whether the lady of the house was called Penny or not, he can't remember.

Bonnington, the cat, comes from a road name close to our old house in Leicester, even though Lucy claims, in *The Fire Within*, that he is named after Chris Bonington, the climber (who incidentally spells his version with a single "n").

Mr. Bacon is a serious nod to Mr. Curry in the *Paddington* books, written by Michael Bond. Chris absolutely adores these. In fact, Paddington is hands down his favorite children's book character.

Zanna was picked up when Chris signed a book for someone of that name, as was Godith. The girl in question pronounced it *God*ith, with the emphasis on the first syllable, but Chris changed the pronunciation to Go*dith* in the books. Either way, a superlative find.

Grockle, the modern-day natural dragon, has an onomatopoeic name, that is, he makes that sound when he tries (and fails) to produce fire.

Gadzooks couldn't have been called anything else. It's a magical name for a magical dragon. Besides which, he wrote it on his pad, so Chris couldn't mistake it.

The name Glade, another of the Pennykettle dragons, was suggested by a girl who e-mailed Chris. She just thought it would be a good choice, as it begins with a G. Chris thought so, too, but had to wait a long time for her to make an appearance in the story. When she did, it was the perfect name for her, and again, couldn't have been anything else.

Lono, a mother polar bear, was "pinched" from a man who wrote a book about them, again as a tribute. It is his last name.

In some cases Chris's characters have been based on the personalities of people he knows or has seen, rather than their names. For instance, Russ, the helicopter pilot for the Polar Research Station in Chamberlain, is loosely based on a working cowboy and musician that we know, who goes by the name of Austin Dan. And, believe it or not, Tam Farrell's entire dress sense is based on a man featured on a fashion makeover show! Chris was so impressed with the jacket that the stylist provided this man with, that he not only went out and bought an identical one for himself, but wrote it into the story. He still has it to this day.

5. WHAT'S WHAT: THE GLOSSARY

There are quite a lot of words in the series that are either obscure, in a foreign language, or simply made up by Chris. The following list should help you understand them all. Most are fully explained in the text as you come to them, so no need to think that you have to have a degree in languages and a memory the size of a planet to enjoy the books. You don't. But here's a general note: The Co:pern:icans use a lot of colons in their language, but almost all of their words are exactly the same in meaning as those we are familiar with in English. For instance — re:gressive, tele:scope, mech:anism. Only those that are substantially different in meaning have been included below.

auma — an Inuit word meaning "fire"; Chris, however, uses it in the Last Dragon Chronicles to mean inner spirit or animating force, the fire within. Dragons are the animating spirit of the natural world. The more auma something has, the more lively or creative it is, and the closer to Gaia it becomes. Auma can be sensed, "read," followed by someone sensitive to it, or raised, usually by specific intention and focus of thought.

aumatic — containing or responsive to auma.

bonglers — everyday name for wind chimes with a relatively low note. As opposed to chinklers, those with a higher-pitched or tinklier sound.

Ci:pherel — a natural dragon who can "read" a person's auma and thereby detect whether they are telling the truth, or are who they claim to be.

coelacanthis — stasis; a state of suspended animation.

Cluster — an Ix assassin, consisting of a few to a multitude of negative Fain entities. Also called **Comm:Ix** or **Ix-risor**.

commingle — to mingle or mix together. Used in the series to mean a conjoining of minds, or of whole personalities, usually involving an entity from a race of beings called the Fain.

Comm:Ix — see **Cluster**.

:coms — communications that are the equivalent to our e-mail, telephone, or video. Also called **e:coms, t:coms,** or **v:coms**.

construct — an imagineered being, in all other respects the equivalent of a human person, animal, or item.

dark fire — the most destructive force in the Universe. Can be brought into being only by an inversion of a source of spiritual purity, such as a selfless act of love, or a moment of inspired creativity. A dragon born of dark fire would be a monster, known as a darkling.

darklings and **semi-darklings** — semi-darklings are potential antidragons, created and controlled by the Ix. They have no separate volition of their own. Attempts to delumine them, i.e., give them independent life via the introduction of dark fire, thereby making them into full darklings, prove fruitless until the events of *The Fire Ascending.*

delumination — the means by which semi-darklings would be brought to independent life as full darklings, via the introduction of dark fire.

digi:grafs — digitally created photographs.

dream it — a phrase used predominantly by Liz Pennykettle to lull someone into a state of relaxation so they can "live" what she is telling them, rather than just imagine it.

fain — on Co:pern:ica, a creative energy possessed by all, and used to imagineer constructs.

Fain, the — a race of thought-beings who have no physical body and exist in another dimension. They have the ability to commingle with any physical life form, the ideal being that of a dragon. This latter, highly desirable achievement is called illumination.

firebird — creature between a dragon and a bird in looks and temperament.

Fire Eternal, the — another name for love, and as such, the title of a book of poems written by Tam Farrell. Also the spiritual fire (white fire) at the center of the Earth, the source from which every natural dragon in this world springs. The greatest creative force in the Universe.

fire star — a portal used by the Fain and the Ix to travel between their world and the Earth. It had been out of alignment with the Earth for a very long time, but is coming into an appropriate position once again by the time of the third book, *Fire Star.*

fire tear — a single tear cried by a dragon immediately before it dies. All the fire that was within the creature is contained in this tear, which falls off its snout onto the ground. It then finds its way back to the fire at the center of the Earth, from whence it originated. A dragon can be made to cry its fire tear before its due time by not loving it, or by otherwise making it extremely sad.

fire within, the — see **auma.**

fluenced — influenced, caused to do as intended by means of magicks.

fosh — Lucy's way of referring to fish. Taken from Allan Ahlberg's book *Ten in a Bed.*

fraas — sparks shed when a dragon's fire tear is produced just before its death. At the place where it lands, its energy will linger; benefits may accrue to any who touch it.

Gaia — the principle that the Earth is a living and breathing entity in its own right, with needs, feelings, desires, and intentions of its (her) own. She works in spirit form to keep the Earth in balance and has, in Chris's books, the ability to bring this about by appearing in many different guises, as circumstances demand, to those who can see her. As they help her, so she in turn helps them. Also called **Gaia principle** or **Mother Earth**.

gardenaria — a construct similar to a human-world garden. It may be changed around or added to simply by desiring it so, and holding that intention.

Grand Design — the Higher's overall plan for Co:pern:ica and its citizens.

Great Re:duction — the loss of plant and animal life on Co:pern:ica caused by too much imagineering by its population.

healing horse — a unicorn.

helegas screen — Co:pern:ican TV/computer outlet, which can also be projected straight onto a wall.

icefire — the substance with which Liz Pennykettle makes her clay dragons come to life. Given to her as a "snowball" when she was a young child.

illumination — the result of the commingling of a Fain entity with a natural dragon. A highly desired spiritual goal and achievement.

i:lluminus and **i:sola** — the former is the illuminated being comprised of a Fain entity and a natural dragon, while they are commingled. The latter refers to the dragon element only of the pair, when the two are physically separated.

imagineer — to create and manifest objects and even people by mental power and intention alone.

inua — soul, inner self.

Inuit — native peoples of the Arctic regions, meaning "the people."

Inuk — the singular form of Inuit, meaning "a man" or "a person."

inversion — positive emotion such as love transformed into negative emotion such as fear, and used against enemies of the Ix, traditionally the Fain and their natural dragons, but now encompassing human beings also. The Ix's intention is to induce humans into negative thought patterns and despair (such as believing there is no hope for the world to solve its problems of pollution, global warming, etc.), so that they can use these to power their semi-darklings, and ultimately to fuel a full darkling. Inner white fire turned into dark fire.

i:sola — see **i:lluminus**.

isoscele — the final triangular scale of a dragon's tail.

Ix, the — the negative element of the Fain; a breakaway group. They wish to gain control of the dark energy of the Universe.

Ix:risor — see **Cluster**.

kabluna — white man; white person.

katt — feline similar to Earth cat, kitten. Also called **kitt-katt**.

Ki:mera — the thought-world inhabited by the Fain and the Ix in a different dimension from the Earth.

krofft — homestead.

librarium — a real building holding millions of real books (i.e., not constructs), looked after by a curator.

mark of Oomara — a symbol of power which can be used for good or evil. The three jagged parallel lines of it represent the lives of men, bears, and dragons — always running alongside each other, but never meeting. The mark, wherever it is found (on Zanna's arm or emblazoned on a polar bear's head, for example) brings an expansion of consciousness. Can be a blessing or a curse.

minits — minutes in Co:pern:ican time.

motested — meeting house.

moyles — the final rows of teeth at the back of a natural dragon's jaws.

mukluks — Arctic boots, made of skins, often trimmed with fur.

nanuk — polar bear.

nanukapik — literally "greatest bear." A leader from the ancient times when dynasties of bears ruled the ice and lived in packs.

natural dragon — a real dragon, large and fire-breathing, as opposed to Liz Pennykettle's clay dragons.

nauja — seagull.

Naunty or **Nunky** — everyday expressions of Aunty and Uncle, used by Lucy, and later by Alexa.

WHAT'S WHAT: THE GLOSSARY

obsidian — a volcanic rock from which the Ix intend to create their darklings.

parthenogenesis — means of reproduction using only an unfertilized egg. How Liz and Lucy were created.

portal — gateway able to be used for time or distance travel.

Premen — early group of beings comprising of a Fain entity commingled with a human being. They ruled the Earth in those far-off days.

Prem:Ix — a human being permanently commingled with an Ix entity.

Pri:magon — a priestess.

properly — the series uses the normal definition of this word, but a note here to say that Lucy uses it grammatically incorrectly. This is deliberate, as part of her character.

puffle — descriptive term for some of the Pennykettle dragons, including Gloria, the dragon on the toilet tank in the bathroom who "puffles" a nice rose scent in place of a more traditional type of air freshener.

qannialaaq — falling snow.

secs — seconds in Co:pern:ican time.

semi-darklings — see **darklings**.

SETH — an acronym for Spatial Enigma and Time Horizons, it refers to an analytical computer program that can detect whether time-slips have occurred, and the probabilities of "portals" being available to use for the purposes of time travel, etc.

sibyl — wise woman, prophetess, witch.

snuffler — descriptive term for some of the Pennykettle dragons, including Gwillan, who as part of his household duties snuffles up dust (as an alternative to a vacuum cleaner), but then puffles out the dust, as ash, later.

spins — Co:pern:ican "years."

spiracle — part of the ventilation system of a dragon, which can be closed at will.

Stencilla — the template used by the Higher to design their perfect society.

stig — retractable thorn that decorates an adult natural dragon's skeleton, particularly along the wings.

taliriktug — strong arm.

therma:sol sheet — an imagineered and therefore pleasantly warm — or cool, as desired — fabric.

third eye — the pineal gland, alleged to be a channel of creative energy, the focus of extra senses (the "sixth sense" and more) in humans and other beings.

time nexus — an unseen field that spatially connects the three worlds of Earth, Ki:mera, and Co:pern:ica. Creatures familiar with the "enchantments of time" (such as dragons, unicorns, and firebirds) have the ability to open portals between these worlds and therefore "Travel" across the nexus.

tornaq — a talisman of fortunes, the correct use of which enables insight into one's true path of destiny. In the books, this particular talisman is a piece of narwhal tusk, a variant form of a birdlike dragon called Groyne. Groyne can freely morph into different shapes, become invisible at will, and Travel through time and space, along with anyone who happens to be holding him, when in his tornaq form.

unnatural eye — an eye in which there is a deliberate defect in the duct, in every natural dragon. This is a kind of sac, a safety mechanism, in one eye only, that won't allow the whole fire tear to pass. A dragon shedding its tear in this way will always retain a little of its spark, and thus be enabled to hibernate for many thousands of years until the tear has fully regenerated.

Wearle — a dragon colony.

wearling — a young dragon belonging to and brought up in a dragon colony.

white fire — "the fire that melts no ice." The title of a book written by David Rain. Also see **Fire Eternal, the**.

whuffler — descriptive term for some of the Pennykettle dragons. They are responsible for the "central heating," given that there are no radiators to be seen anywhere at number 42 Wayward Crescent.

wuzzled — sleepy or dazed.

wuzzled off — went to sleep, or a gentle euphemism for "died," depending on the context. Usually used with regard to animals, but can be expanded to include humans.

6. WHERE'S WHERE: THE SETTINGS

Chris is often asked why, if the Last Dragon Chronicles is a fantasy saga, most of it is set in the real world of day-to-day life, but where magical things happen. He has two answers to that. One is that the squirrel story at the heart of the first book, *The Fire Within*, is necessarily set in such a world, and so everything else had to be; the other is that he was initially very wary about creating something "other," given his then rather poor track history of attempting to write science fiction stories. His confidence has grown considerably since (read *Fire World*, for instance!), but the scene was set (or rather, the scenes were set) beyond any substantial change long before that point. Perhaps there is a third reason — that he simply thoroughly enjoys writing family drama–type scenarios. It's what he relishes most of all.

Although there are many, many settings throughout the series, these can be largely separated into three distinct groupings. These are Earth (modern day and, paradoxically, in the last book in the series, in early times), Ki:mera, and Co:pern:ica. As Ki:mera, the home thought-world of the Fain, is never actually seen, it obviously cannot be described here. Co:pern:ican settings are entirely fictitious and not based on any particular places currently in existence. Many of the Earth settings, however, are recognizable as specific locations around the world. As Chris lives in England, most of them can be found there. When the Last Dragon Chronicles was published in the US, though, it seemed natural to relocate some of the settings to North America, as you will see.

SCRUBBLEY

Scrubbley is, as already mentioned, a thinly-disguised Bromley, in Kent, England. In the United States,

Scrubbley is a fictitious town in Massachusetts, near Boston. Number 42 Wayward Crescent is a traditional 1930s house. Lucy's room faces the road at the front of the house. David's room is on the ground floor and faces onto the backyard, where much of the action featuring Henry Bacon, who lives in the house next door, occurs. Most of the domestic scenes within the Pennykettle household center around the kitchen and the Dragons' Den, the studio where Liz makes her clay creations:

All around the studio, arranged on tiers of wooden shelves, were dozens and dozens of handcrafted dragons. There were big dragons, little dragons, dragons curled up in peaceful slumber, baby dragons breaking out of their eggs, dragons in spectacles, dragons in pajamas, dragons doing ballet, dragons everywhere. Only the window wall didn't have a rack. Over there, instead, stood a large old bench. A lamp was angled over it. There were brushes and tools and jelly jars prepared, plus lumps of clay beside a potter's wheel.

The sweet smell of paint and methyl acetate hung in the air like a potpourri aroma.

The scent of potpourri also hangs in the air in Zanna's New Age shop, The Healing Touch. She bought this property with the aid of royalties from David's two commercially successful books after he was lost in the Arctic, presumed dead. Liz helps her with child-care duties so that Zanna can work on building the shop up from scratch. The shop layout was inspired by that of a local health-food store, though the latter is a bit smaller than Zanna's business and has neither an upstairs open to the public nor a potions dragon to assist in making up the tinctures.

The previous owner had run the property as a small gift shop and had passed it on with all the fixtures in place. Pine shelving racks occupied the two long walls and a glass display counter faced the door. Behind it, curtained off by bamboo strips, were two utility areas that served as stock room, preparation room, and kitchen. The two rooms upstairs were bare and dusty, but over the next three years, as her turnover increased and her reputation for producing effective "lotions and potions" expanded, Zanna was able to decorate throughout and turn them into her consulting area, for clients requiring her unique brand of healing.

Tam Farrell, a journalist who is investigating David Rain's mysterious disappearance in the Arctic, buys a clay dragon from Zanna's shop one day and invites her to attend a poetry reading at Allandale's bookshop in an attempt to win her trust and get her to open up to him. This bookshop is based on one called Browsers, which used to be situated in Allandale Road in Leicester, England, but is sadly now closed; Sandra, who co-owned it, became Cassandra in the books.

It was the same room, set out in just the same way, with three arcs of soft-backed chairs and a small lectern at the front. The main ceiling lights had been turned off, and the room was illuminated by filtered blue halogens built into the two walls of bookshelves. Ten or a dozen people were already randomly seated, poring over programs, but Zanna's eye was drawn to a larger group, clustered around a table where tea and fruit juice were being served. She spotted Tam Farrell in quiet conversation with a spiky-haired woman, whom she knew to be the bookshop owner, Cassandra.

Zanna is distraught and very angry when she discovers that Tam is only befriending her because of his professional interest in David. However, when she is attacked by semi-darklings, on a place called North Walk, it is Tam who rescues her and thus becomes a trusted companion after all. In real life, North Walk is the image of a beautiful tree-lined avenue in Leicester called New Walk, which runs from the heart of the city to a lovely open park next to the university. It's exactly as described prior to the attack scenes, even including the museum and double-mouthed mailbox — but minus semi-darklings and Tam Farrell.

New Walk in Leicester, the inspiration for North Walk

[North Walk] was a wide asphalt path that cut through the professional heart of Scrubbley. The houses that ran along one side were mostly occupied by lawyers or accountants. . . . Alexa preferred the other side of North Walk. There were houses and offices along here, too, and a fine museum of art. But dotted between the buildings were squares and rectangles of urban grassland, shaded by vast maple and oak trees. Lucy had once written a story for school about two squirrels that lived on the edge of such a square. The name of

107

the story was "Bodger and Fuffle from Twenty-three Along." The number twenty-three referred to the broken glass lantern, on the twenty-third lamppost from the top end of the Walk, where the squirrels had built their home. One of Alexa's favorite games was to count the lampposts aloud, even though she knew exactly which one (by the double-mouthed blue mailbox just beyond the museum) was home to the legendary squirrels.

Not far from the park end of New Walk, Rutherford House (previously a lunatic asylum, in the books) is based on a slightly adapted part of Leicester University's campus, which, incidentally, shared the same history before it became an educational establishment.

Although Caractacus the crow attacks Conker the squirrel in the garden at 42 Wayward Crescent in the Last Dragon Chronicles, the idea for this scene was implanted in Chris's mind many years before in the graveyard adjacent to another part of the university campus — the Medical School's parking lot. This is where Chris worked for twenty-eight years, before becoming

Conker's sanctuary

a full-time writer. The Med School, not the parking lot, of course.

One day, he was called outside by a friend to witness (and try to capture) a gray squirrel running around in wide circles, obviously trying to escape from something but unable to move in a straight line. It transpired that a crow had made a lunge at it, for reasons unknown, and damaged one of its eyes. Despite a crazy half hour with Chris running around after it with an empty cardboard box, it did eventually manage to get itself away from both the crow and Chris, and finally disappeared under the fence and among the graves. Chris followed in hot pursuit, but never saw it again. The image and the memory stayed with him for over a decade before ultimately being written into literary history.

BEYOND SCRUBBLEY

A little farther afield, the location of the Old Gray Dragon guest house, where Lucy and Tam stay in *Dark Fire*, was based on a bed-and-breakfast that Chris and I stayed at in Glastonbury, England, right at the foot of the Tor. A tor is a small hill, and the one at Glastonbury is a major tourist attraction. The owners of the bed-and-breakfast were a wonderfully welcoming couple and absolutely nothing like the characters of Hannah and Clive, who own the Old Gray Dragon in the book. The back door of the guesthouse opened onto a private path that led onto the public one and thence right to the top of the Tor.

Once at the top of the Tor (called Glissington Tor in the novels), and with Tam's help, Lucy surveys the land with the intent of raising a natural dragon that she believes has been in stasis for hundreds of years, somewhere beneath their feet. Opposite the Tor is another hill, Scuffenbury, where there is a chalk horse etched into the grass. It is alleged that when moonlight falls in a particular way on the horse's head, the dragon will awaken, but Hannah later suggests to Lucy that there is a better and easier way to achieve that — by touching the dragon itself. To this end, Hannah guides Tam and Lucy through some tunnels under the Tor which have been professionally excavated in years gone by, abandoned, then later extended by her husband.

In real life, the horse on Scuffenbury Hill is based on the white chalk horse at Uffington, in Oxfordshire, England. Glissington Tor itself, although based mainly upon Glastonbury Tor (especially for shape and size), is further influenced by the man-made mound at Silbury, in Wiltshire, England. It is at this site that excavations were professionally made. Nothing unexpected was found there. When it came time to "move" Scuffenbury Hill to its new location for the US edition of the Chronicles, however, there was a slight snag: There are no chalk hills anywhere in the United States!

Therefore one was created specially, in (very appropriately) New England. Maine, you now have a new tourist attraction. . . .

Farther afield again, and in London now (US version: Boston), both in the books and in real life, Apple Tree Publishing (the company that publishes David's books) is highly reminiscent of Chris's UK publisher's old offices. . . .

The offices of Apple Tree Publishing were wedged between a lumberyard and a bar in a cramped and rundown area of Boston. It was hardly the castle of literary elegance that David Rain had imagined it to be. Redevelopment was everywhere. Half the road was checkered by scaffolding. Boards surrounded the knocked-out shop fronts. The smell of damp brick dust hung in the air. Taxicabs shuttled past, squirting slush onto the snow-packed sidewalks. And from every quarter there came a noise. Hammering, drilling, workers shouting, music thumping out of the bar, the steady buzz of traffic, the rumble of a bus, the sucking whistle of an overhead plane.

... and *The National Endeavor* newspaper offices, where Tam Farrell works, of the UK publisher's new ones.

According to Gwendolen's place-finding search engine, the offices of The National Endeavor *were in a large glass building on Cambridge Street, half a mile's walk from the T station. On her map, the thick green line of the highway did not appear especially intimidating, but even though Lucy was no stranger to Boston, the pace of life here in the rush hour frightened her. Cambridge Street was a busy four-lane highway, yet there was traffic congestion on one side of the road, made worse by a fire truck and a clutch of police cars, which were throwing their red lights into the rain.... She just pulled up her collar and hurried on past.... By now, if her bearings were correct, she should be right near the magazine's offices. A truck powered by, rattling every pane of glass in sight. Then a horn blared, making her squeal in fright, driving her toward a revolving door. She saw the word* Endeavor *and just kept on moving, glad to let it carry her out of the noise.*

Incidentally, the character of Dilys Whutton, who appears in *Fire Star*, is an homage to one of Chris's previous editors, though he won't allow me to say which one! Probably scared he'll never be invited to "do lunch" ever again.

David's home address, 4 Thousall Road, Blackburn, Lancashire (4 Thousall Road, Blackburn, Massachusetts, in the US editions), is another Beatles reference, from a song called "A Day in the Life," which mentions something along the lines of there being four thousand holes in Blackburn, Lancashire.

INTO THE ARCTIC

The Arctic settings (including those mentioned in *The Fire Ascending* relating to the early days on Earth) are much more generalized, and not often tied to any specific real-life places. The mountainous region of Kasgerden, the Horste and Skoga forests, and the Bridge of Taan are all entirely from Chris's imagination. The one notable exception to this is modern-day

Chamberlain, which is (*very* loosely) based on the existence of a town named Churchill in Manitoba, Canada. This is somewhere that Chris would love to visit because, for part of the year, polar bears gather there in large numbers, waiting for the sea ice to freeze sufficiently so that they can go out to hunt seal, their staple diet. Whether he'll be welcome there after the inhabitants read his version of life in that neck of the woods is anybody's guess.

"Neck of the woods" isn't a particularly appropriate phrase to use, in truth, as "woods" or even single trees are almost nonexistent in that area because the weather conditions are not temperate enough for them to survive. Here's a passage from *Fire Star* that gives you a flavor of this remote Arctic setting:

[Zanna] dropped the parking brake and gunned the truck forward. Its rear wheels squealed as they bit the road. Snowflakes as large as lemons hit the screen and were quickly swept aside into a layer of slush. Zanna shifted her gaze to the east. Out toward open

water, surrounded by dirt stacks and rusting junked machinery, lay the moody hulk of the grain elevator, a large white ocean liner of a building, blackened with smoke from a nearby chimney, splashed against the bleak gray Manitoba sky. For eight months of the year, when the bay was clear of ice, Chamberlain fed the north with grain. The sight of it reminded her why they'd come. "Got your list?"

David unflapped a pocket. . . . The romantic in him had wanted to see a bygone time of people in furs outside their igloos, chewing skins and dressing kayaks. But the latter-day reality wasn't even close. The "igloos" were rows of painted wooden buildings, mostly squat residential cabins. The only suggestion of a native heritage was a parka-clad figure attending a dog team. The man had a cigarette hanging off his lip and two curtains of black hair sprouting shabbily from under his cap. The dogs, despite the unflagging cold, seemed as happy as a small flock of sheep in a summer field.

As they turned into the center of the town, David

was reminded that one of the principal attractions of Chamberlain was its tourist industry. People came here to photograph bears. There were several gift shops testifying to it, plus an Inuit museum he'd heard Russ and Dr. Bergstrom talk about. On its wall was a sign declaring, FIVE CITIZENS FOR EVERY BEAR. He took this to mean that the town's population was approximately one thousand, as he knew from his studies that somewhere around two hundred bears passed through Chamberlain annually. Yellow warning signs were everywhere, reminding people of it.

BE ALERT!
POLAR BEAR SEASON
October thru November
Memorize this number

The number in question was the polar bear "police." If any bad guys lumbered in, Chamberlain, it seemed, was ready to run them out of town.

Most of the other scenes are just out on the ice, nearer or farther away from various real areas, though Chris has invented a village called Savalik, which is where Tootega, an Inuit worker at the Polar Research Station a few days' journey away, was born and brought up.

A modern settlement of twenty or thirty large wooden houses, it mirrored Chamberlain in all but size. It was snowbound on three sides, the houses huddled in a cloistered heap like Christmas presents on a large white armchair. Tootega, when he saw it this time, was reminded of something David Rain had said about Inuit settlements looking like a room that you forgot to clean. Anything an Inuk did not need, any broken-down appliance or unused item, he would cast away — but not very far. So it was in Savalik. An incongruous mix of brightly painted roofs and over-hanging wires and old oil barrels and junked bent metal and columns of steam. But it was home, and the dogs knew it, too. Their noses lifted at the first scent of seal meat warming in a pot. Their tails wagged.

Their paws spent less time in contact with the ice. Orak, the lead dog, whose mapping was every bit as sensitive as his master's, was tugging his comrades toward the colony long before the whip was up.

Tootega has come to visit his grandfather, who is very ill, in his home in the settlement. Nauja, Tootega's sister-in-law, is looking after the old man.

Tootega went in, bowing his head. The old man, famed throughout the north as a healer and shaman, commanded great respect within the community and even more esteem at home. He gave a thin cry of joy to see his firstborn grandson and called out to Nauja, Mattak! Mattak! meaning she should bring them whale meat to chew. Tootega crossed the floor, surprised to find a woolen rug under his feet. It dismayed him every time he came to this house to see his grandfather a little more absorbed by southern culture. This room, with its wardrobes and lampshades and remote-controlled television, was a painful affliction of the disease called progress. Tootega could readily remember a time when this proud and happy man, now lying in a bed that had drawers in the mattress and propped up loosely on a cluster of pillows, would have been surrounded by furs and harpoons and a seal oil lamp, with blood and blubber stains under his feet. On the wall above the bed, slightly tilted at an angle, was a framed embroidered picture saying "Home, Sweet Home" in the Inuit language. To see it made Tootega want to empty his gut.

Progress will always happen, in the High Arctic as well as everywhere else, of course. And this is not necessarily a bad thing. However, Chris is deeply concerned about the effects of pollution, global warming, climate change, and so on, especially regarding polar bears, one of his favorite animals. So much so, that he has David, working at the research base already mentioned, write in a letter back home to Liz and Lucy:

We spend our days analyzing ice samples. Some of them date back hundreds of years. Zanna is checking for increases in toxic chemicals called PCBs, which can poison bears and other forms of wildlife, and I am melting ice cores down and making the tea — I mean, making interesting graphs to monitor the levels of something called beryllium 10. This is to do with global warming. Dr. Bergstrom thinks that changes in the levels of beryllium 10 coincide with an increase in sunspots or flares, which might be warming the Earth and making the polar ice cap melt. That's scary, especially for bears. Every year, the ice in Hudson Bay melts earlier but takes a little longer to refreeze. This means that bears are fasting more and more and will reach a point, maybe in the next fifty years, when they will not be able to survive their time ashore and will die of starvation out on the tundra. It's hard to believe that the natural world we take so much for granted is constantly under threat from climatic change and that creatures like polar bears could so easily become extinct. No one here wants to see that happen. So we are busy searching for long-term answers, feeding the data into our computers to try to predict how long the polar ice will last.

So how can you and I make a difference? David writes *White Fire*, of course, to bring these issues to the attention of the public. But Chris feels that such a grand gesture may not be necessary. He believes (and has David and Tam Farrell believe, too) that a solution to global warming can be achieved with a single sentence: *Make polar bears an endangered species.* Tell this to the big industrial nations. If they approve it, they will be forced to protect the beasts' icy habitat, and in doing so, they might just save the world.

7. MYTHS AND LEGENDS

One of Chris's few clear memories of his school days is being fascinated by the ancient stories of gods, kings, and mere mortals as told by the Greeks and Romans. He has had a love for myth, legend, and parable ever since. The opportunity to create a few of his own, therefore, was just too good to miss.

Instead of stories about flying too close to the sun or leaving threads through mazes, however, most of Chris's center around polar bears and dragons — with a few sibyls thrown in for good measure. He did come across one genuine old Inuit tale along the way, and that is the story of Sedna, the sea goddess. This made such an impression on him that he decided to not only include the original legend in *The Fire Eternal,* but also have Sedna appear as a character.

SEDNA

The legend of Sedna was almost as old as the ice itself. Like ice, it had many variations, fashioned by slips of the tongue on the wind. But the version which came to the Teller of Ways as he watched the sea goddess thrash her tail and squirm from her ocean home was this:

She had been a beautiful Inuit woman, courted by many worthy suitors, hunters of strength, agility, and passion, all of whom would have crossed the ice for her, drunk the ocean, sewn the clouds together with spears. But Sedna was vain and refused them all. She preferred to sit by her father's igloo, admiring her reflection in the waters of the ocean, all the while combing her shining dark hair.

One day, her father grew tired of this. He said to her, "My daughter, we are starving. All the animals have deserted us. We do not even have a dog to slay. I am old and too weary to hunt. You must marry the next hunter who comes to our camp or we will be nothing but sacks of bones."

But Sedna ignored him, selfishly, saying, "I am Sedna. I am beautiful. What more do I need?"

Her father despaired, and thought to take a knife to her and use her as bait to trap a passing bear. But the next day, while he sat aboard his sled, sharpening his blade and his will to live, another hunter entered the camp. He was tall and elegantly dressed in furs, but his face was hidden by the trimmings around his hood.

The man said, "I am in need of a wife." He struck the shaft of his spear into the ice, making cracks that ran like claws.

Sedna's father was afraid, but he boldly said, "I have a daughter, a beautiful daughter. She can cook and sew and chew skins to make shirts. What will you give in return for her, hunter?"

"I give fish," said the man, from the darkness of his hood.

"Ai-yah." Sedna's father waved a hand, for he thought it a poor trade: fish — for a daughter! But fish was better than a hole in his stomach. And so he said this, "Tomorrow, bring your kayak, filled with char. Row it to the headland, and I will exchange the char for my daughter."

The hunter made a crackling sound in his throat, but his face did not appear from his hood. He withdrew his spear from the glistening ice, pulling out with it a swirling storm. From the eye of the storm he cried, "So be it." And he was gone, as if the wind had claimed him like a feather.

That night, Sedna's father made up a potion, a sleeping potion squeezed from the bloodshot eye of a walrus, that laziest of Arctic creatures. This he stirred into a warming broth, made from the boiled skin of his mukluks, his boots. "Come, daughter," he said, singing sweetly in her ear. "Come, eat with your aged father." And he gave Sedna a bowl of his broth to drink. Within moments, she had fallen asleep at his feet. Her father then wrapped her loosely in furs and in the morning carried her out to his sled. Still she slept on as he tied her to it, unaware of the trade that awaited her. But there was little remorse in her father's heart. For Sedna was idle, and char were char. With a great heave, he pulled her away from their camp. She had still not woken by the time they reached the headland.

The hunter stood by his kayak, waiting. Its skins were bulging, brim-full with fish. Their dead eyes watched a soulless father unload his daughter and roll her out at the hunter's feet. The hunter made a chirring sound in his throat. He told the old man to empty the kayak. The Inuk, driven by greed and stupidity, gathered too many fish in his arms, and slipped and skidded and fell upon his back. As his head struck the ice his gluttonous gaze softened. His dizzied brain recoiled in horror as he watched the hunter pick up his only child, grow a pair of wings, and fly away with her to a distant cliff! "Come back!" he cried, and reached out a hand. A fish slithered out of it and lodged in his mouth. It was rotten from the tailbone through to the eye.

When Sedna awoke she found herself lying in a nest of hair and night-black feathers. She was on a high ledge, surrounded by ravens. Far below her, the sea was rushing at the rocks, dashing itself to foam and spray. "Oh, my father! Help me! Help!" she cried. Then appeared by her side the hunter who had claimed her.

"I am your husband now," he said.

And he threw off his furs to show himself to be a raven. The king of ravens. The darkest of birds.

Sedna screamed and screamed, until her voice broke to the cark of a bird. Her fear was so great that the north wind wrestled with her terror for weeks, finally carrying it howling to her father. It beat about his ears, his soul, his heart. How could you do this? *it whistled at him.* How could you marry your daughter to a bird? Do you want to be known as the grandfather of ravens?

The old man was wracked with sadness and guilt. He chattered to his heart and his heart chattered back. He must go out and rescue his daughter, it said.

So, the very next morning, he loaded up his patched old kayak and paddled through the frigid Arctic waters, until he reached the cliff that was Sedna's new home. Sedna, who now had eyes as sharp as any bird, had seen him coming and was waiting at the shore. "Oh, my father," she said and hugged him tightly, smelling his furs, which still reeked of fish.

"Quickly," he said, "while the mist is about us." And they climbed into his kayak and paddled away.

They had traveled for many hours and still had the calm of the ocean all about them when Sedna saw a black speck high in the sky. Fear welled up inside her, for she knew this was her husband coming to find her!

"Paddle faster!" she urged her father.

But her father's arms were slow with age and exhaustion. The raven was upon their boat as swiftly as a ray of sunlight. It swooped down and set the kayak bobbing. "Give me back my wife!" it screamed.

Sedna's father struck at the thing with his paddle.

He missed and almost fell into the water. "Trickster be gone!" he shouted in vain.

The bird caarked *in anger and swooped again. This time it came down low to the water, beating one wing against the surface. A ferocious storm began to blow and the waters became a raging torrent, tossing the kayak to and fro. Sedna screamed, but not as loudly as her father. Once more, cowardice had rooted in his heart. With a mighty shove, he pushed his daughter into the ocean. "Be gone! Leave me be! Here is your precious wife!" he cried. "Take her back and trouble me no more!"*

Sedna cried out in disbelief. "Father, do not desert me!" she begged. She swam to the kayak and reached up, grasping the side of the boat. But the icy waters had made her arms numb and she could not haul herself back to safety.

Still the raven plunged and swooped. The storm grew worse. In his madness, Sedna's father saw a shoal of rotten char coming to the surface to feed, if he fell.

Addled by terror, he grabbed his kayak paddle once more and pounded Sedna's fingers with it. She wailed in agony but he would not stop. "Take her! Take her!" he shouted crazily, believing that the only way to save his life was to sacrifice his daughter's life instead. Over and over again he struck, until one by one, her frozen fingers cracked. They dropped into the ocean where they turned into seals and small whales as they sank. With her hands broken, Sedna could not hold on to the boat. Her mutilated body slipped under the water and slowly faded out of sight. . . .

. . . Yet, she did not perish. Poisoned by the magic of a raven's bile and further tormented by unresolved grief, she made her house at the bottom of the sea, where she became the goddess of the ocean, raging at men through violent storms. . . .

If you want to know why David Rain calls the now terrifying, rather than terrified, Sedna up from her home at the bottom of the ocean, and what he has to offer her to get her aid, you'll have to read the book! (In this instance, *The Fire Eternal*, the fourth in the series.)

CHRIS'S MYTHS AND LEGENDS

The following pages relate several snippets from some of Chris's own myths and legends, but so your enjoyment of the books won't be spoiled, I won't tell you the endings. Sorry! An extract from Lucy's journal would be a good place to start.

My name is Lucy. Lucy Pennykettle. I'm sixteen. I turn heads. I get noticed. A lot. Mainly for the bright green eyes and mass of red hair. I live in a leafy little town called Scrubbley with my mom, Liz, and her partner, Arthur, and my part-sister, Zanna, and her sweet kid, Alexa. My cat, Bonnington, is the weirdest feline you'll ever meet. We share the house with a bunch of special dragons, like the one sitting next to my keyboard, Gwendolen. Dragons. More about them in a mo.

Arthur (wise stepdad, sort of) told me once that people believe what they see in print. So here are a few small truths about me, just to get things into perspective:

My favorite food is vanilla-flavored yogurt.

I'm slightly scared of moths.

Squirrels break my heart.

I think I'm in love with a guy named Tam.

I'm totally in awe of the author David Rain.

I'm worried about the mist that's covering the Arctic.

I'm haunted by the shadow of beings called the Ix.

But there's one thing that keeps me awake most nights, and lately I can't wrap my head around it:

I look like a girl. I think like a girl. I walk and talk like a girl.

But I was not born the way other girls are.

I hatched — from an egg.

I

AM

NOT

HUMAN

One of the *special* dragons, Gadzooks, eventually goes to visit a man named Professor Steiner and writes something on one of the professor's parchments:

He crossed over to his desk and unlocked a drawer. From it he withdrew a single sheet of paper. It appeared to be made of thick gray cotton, like a small hand towel stiffened with starch. He passed it first to Lucy, who glanced at the pen marks and said, with disappointment, "It looks like a doodle."

"Many ancient languages do," said Arthur. "If you'd never seen Japanese or Arabic writing you would probably not associate the characters with the words at first. What do you make of it, Elizabeth?"

134

She took the paper and examined it. "I see what Lucy means. There doesn't appear to be a formal phonetic structure. Though the strokes suggest it. They're very deliberate."

"I agree," said Rupert Steiner, buoyed by her assessment, "but it's quite unlike anything I've interpreted before. I couldn't even guess at its country of origin. The frustrating thing is, I'm sure I've seen another example of this, but I can't place it."

"Could it be a drawing, perhaps?" Arthur asked.

The professor rubbed the question into his cheek. "The recording of history through storytelling and drawing was prevalent in our earliest ancestors, but even the wildest imagination couldn't pull these marks into a meaningful picture. No, I'm convinced it's a text of some kind."

"Can I have another look?" Lucy took the page onto her knees again, turning it through several angles. "It reminds me a bit of the marks I saw on a wall in that cave on the Tooth of Ragnar."

"The Tooth of Ragnar?" Steiner jerked back as if

he'd been shot. "You've been there? But that island is — or rather was — in one of the remotest parts of the Arctic. Were you taken there on a school trip or something?"

"Erm . . . something," Lucy replied, putting the sheet down on the coffee table. Her mind flashed back five years to when she'd been abducted by Gwilanna and taken to the island as a part of the sibyl's bungled attempt to raise Gawain from the dead. Many times she'd been left to fend for herself, with nothing but wild mushrooms to eat and a female polar bear for company. That had been one heck of a "school trip."

"How extraordinary," Rupert said. "You must have been awfully young. You were lucky to visit it before it was destroyed by volcanic activity. The Tooth of Ragnar is a fascinating place, steeped in all sorts of Inuit myth. Why —"

"Just a moment, Professor." Liz cut him off and turned her attention to Gwendolen, who'd just given out a startled hurr. The little dragon was on the coffee table, standing by the sheet of paper.

"What's the matter?" Liz asked her.

The professor steered his gaze between the dragon and the woman. "Goodness! Can you converse with it?"

"Yes," said Liz, without looking up. "Go on, Gwendolen."

Gwendolen stepped forward and pointed to the writing. I know how to read it, *she hurred*.

"How?" said Lucy.

It's dragontongue, *Gwendolen said (rather proudly)*.

Lucy moved her aside. "Dragontongue? I didn't even know you could write it down."

"Me neither," Liz admitted, sitting back, stunned. She glanced at Arthur, who was stroking his chin in what she always called his "pondering" mode.

"Elizabeth's dragons speak a language roughly akin to Gaelic, Rupert. It's possible to learn it, given time."

Steiner bent over the coffee table and peered at Gwendolen as if she were a prize. The dragon warily flicked her tail. She hurred again at length.

"Did she speak then? I thought I saw smoke. And did her eyes also change color?"

"*You're making her nervous,*" *said Liz.* "*She wouldn't normally be allowed to act this freely in human company and you shouldn't, by rights, be able to see her. Somehow, Gadzooks must have made that possible.*"

"*Speaking of which . . .*" *Lucy gestured a hand.*

Liz glanced at the writing again. "*Gwendolen has just explained that the curves on the paper are like the way she moves her throat to make growling sounds.*"

"*Yeah, but what does it say?*" *pressed Lucy.*

Gwendolen gathered her eye ridges together and frowned at the markings again. It was not a word she recognized, she said, but she thought she could speak the pronunciation correctly. She cleared her throat and uttered a long, low hurr.

Lucy glanced at her mother, who gave the translation. "*Scuffenbury,*" *said Liz.*

After a chat with David, Lucy now thinks she knows a bit more about why Gadzooks wrote "Scuffenbury" on Professor Steiner's parchment.

"Scuffenbury" in dragontongue

At the end of the last dragon era, it came to a point where there were just twelve left. Driven from their aeries by wild-hearted men who knew no better than to kill a creature they couldn't tolerate and didn't understand, the dragons came together and decided to surrender. They didn't give themselves up for capture or sacrifice; they just refused to fight anymore. This, to me, is the saddest story ever. I grow tired of people who only think of dragons as fire-breathing, maiden-snatching, cave-dwelling monsters. Dragons had heart. Morals. Courage. Zanna always says they were the spiritual guardians of the Earth, and for once I agree with her. We don't really know what happened to the twelve. The legend is they separated and flew away to isolated places, remote volcanic islands and the like, where they could live out their lives in peace, and where they could eventually die in peace. Up until yesterday, the only location I knew about was the Tooth of Ragnar, where Gawain set down. Now, if David is telling the truth, there's one hidden underneath Glissington Tor, close to Scuffenbury Hill, not a million miles from here.

Professor Steiner has also informed Liz and Lucy that he has seen dragontongue written before — in some photographs of wall markings taken in caves at a place called the Hella glacier. Henry Bacon, the Pennykettles' next-door neighbor, tells David of an incident that happened there when Henry's grandfather was part of an expedition to explore the area in 1913. A fellow explorer had disappeared there in unusual circumstances — lost, presumed dead. Lorel is a polar bear captured in a photograph on the study wall.

"People say he wandered off to find his watch."

"What?"

"Had a risky incident a few months before. Found himself stranded near a native settlement with a large male polar bear for company. No rifle, and too far away from camp to summon help. All he had with him was a pocket watch. Played a tune when you opened the casing. Our fellow set it down in front of the bear. Story goes, the beast swaggered up to the watch, sat down, and listened. Our man backed off and escaped to camp.

141

Went back with his comrades twenty minutes later, but the watch and the bear had both disappeared."

"Who was this man?" David asked nervously.

Henry turned the book around. He pointed to a plate at the bottom of a page. "Third from the left. Fair-haired. Scandinavian."

David cast his eyes down.

It was Dr. Bergstrom.

As David's mind wrestled with the incredible conundrum of how a man in his forties who lectured at Scrubbley College could look exactly like a polar explorer reported missing in 1913, the house came alive with the trill of telephones. David thought he detected four at least. Henry snapped the book shut and returned it to the shelf. "Something amiss, boy? You look a bit pale."

"I'm fine," said David, "just . . . thinking, that's all." He cupped his hand around Gadzooks and looked through the slatted window blinds. There was a good view of the Pennykettles' garden from here. He picked out Lucy right away, still by the brambles, puttering

about with her hedgehog book. A slightly moody-looking Bonnington was sitting near the rock garden, paws tucked under his tummy, watching. And in the center of the lawn, as if a cloud had dripped and left a great white blot, lay the hunk of ice that had once been a snowbear, still surviving despite the rain. As Henry lifted a phone and the house became silent, David thought about Lorel and turned to look at the bear print again. For a fleeting moment he became the bear, looking back into the lens of Bergstrom's camera. And from somewhere between the bear and the man, from the bright cold wilderness of frozen ages, from the leaves of books, from the creaking timbers of icebound vessels, came a voice like a wind from another world, saying, There was a time when the ice was ruled by nine bears . . .

(. . . which is a whole other story: Chris's own massive *White Fire* Arctic saga. But you can read a little more about the nine bears in *Icefire*.)

And finally, I can't close this section without bowing to the wishes of a huge number of fans who have begged

There was a time when the ice was ruled by nine bears....

to know why all the dragons' names begin with a *G*. The answer is in *Dark Fire*, but for those of you who haven't read that far yet, here goes. A little preamble from Arthur first, then the reveal by Gwilanna (she's got to be good for something).

"When I was at the abbey, I had a dream. I saw the universe created from the outgoing breath of a dragon called Godith. Everything was born from the fire of that dragon. A white fire. Auma in its purest sense. You and I, this physical world we inhabit, came into being when the fire cooled down to a low enough vibration to produce ingenious combinations of atoms and molecules."

Hy-dragon, rather then hydrogen, one assumes. Well, we humans nearly got it right!

"The letter G," said Zanna, wishing more than anything she'd brought Gretel with her. The potions dragon would have been working on escape routes from the

start. Moments to live? What was the crazed witch talking about?

"Not just any G," Gwilanna drawled on. "A G curling into an isoscele. It represents the tail of their creator, the she-dragon, Godith. Haven't you ever wondered why dragons copy it into their names? To have the sign of Godith on your breath is a mark of respect. Really, girl, you're such a waste. You could have learned so much from me."

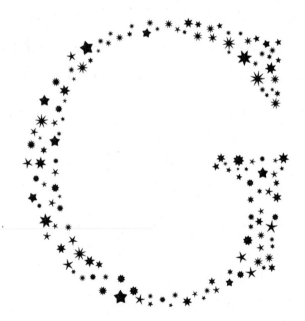

So now you know.

8. The Light and the Dark

The first book in the series, *The Fire Within*, is an apparently simple, straightforward, and charming story about a young man who comes to stay as a tenant with a single-parent family, helps rescue an injured squirrel, and makes the acquaintance of a few clay dragons along the way.

Even if it was that simple, it gives absolutely no clue as to the power and profundity yet to come in the rest of the books. The stories get deeper, darker, and much more complex as they progress, while still retaining their trademark humor — from slapstick to black comedy — even in the direst of circumstances.

The story lines range from cozy domestic drama to an interdimensional war between races of thought-beings, into which humans are in danger of being dragged. There is mystery, danger, and adventure by the bucketload, and this chapter gives a glimpse of what happens in each.

THE FIRE WITHIN

The series starts with David Rain about to move into the Pennykettle household on Wayward Crescent. David is marveling at one of the small clay dragons he has seen all around the house ever since he first walked in the door of Liz and Lucy's home. He does not yet know that they can come to life.

There was a fiery pride in its oval-shaped eyes as if it had a sense of its own importance and knew it had a definite place in the world. Its tall slim body was painted green with turquoise hints at the edges of its scales. It was sitting erect on two flat feet and an arrow-shaped tail that swung back on itself in a single loop. Four ridged wings (two large, two small) fanned

THE LIGHT AND THE DARK

out from its back and shoulders. A set of spiky, flaglike scales ran the entire length of its spine.

David picked it up — and very nearly dropped it. "It's warm," he said, blinking in surprise.

"That's because —"

"It's been in the sun too long," said Mrs. Pennykettle, quickly cutting her daughter off. She lifted the dragon out of David's hands and rested it gently back on the shelf.

David soon learns that Liz Pennykettle makes these dragons, styled in a variety of poses and often with certain characteristics emphasized. She sells some of them at the market in Scrubbley. Liz has a studio in a room upstairs, called the Dragons' Den, and the new tenant is told in no uncertain terms by Lucy that he is not allowed to enter. Needless to say, this piques David's curiosity, but he manages to stifle the impulse to have a sneaky look in, at least for a while.

In the meantime, Lucy, who is very fond of wildlife, implores David to help her to find an injured squirrel

RAIN & FIRE

she has seen in the garden, and which she has named Conker. David agrees after some cajoling, but upon meeting the Pennykettles' next-door neighbor, Henry Bacon, he realizes that he will have competition for this task. Henry's interest in capturing the squirrel is not benevolent, as he believes that squirrels have been responsible for eating his flowers and digging up his bulbs. To this end, he has gotten the town council to chop down a grand old oak tree that used to be home to a whole group of these creatures, which have now disappeared from the area. Only Conker is left behind.

Back in the Dragons' Den, Liz has been making a "special" dragon for David as a housewarming gift. Despite Lucy's dire warning for him to stay out of the studio, Mrs. Pennykettle invites him in, where he gets introduced to several of the small dragons who are resident in the household. David's dragon turns out to be similar to the other dragons, except that it (he) is holding something. . . .

. . . It had a pencil wrapped in its claws and was biting the end of it, lost in thought.

"Hope you like him," said Liz. "He was . . . interesting to do."

"He's wonderful," said David. "Why does he have a pencil?"

"And a pad?" said Lucy, pointing to a notepad in the dragon's other paw.

"It's what he wanted," said Liz, coming to join them. "I tried him with a book, but he just didn't like it. He definitely wanted a pencil to chew on."

"Perhaps he's a drawing dragon," said Lucy. "Do you like drawing pictures?"

David shook his head. "Can't draw for anything. What do you mean, he 'wanted' a pencil?"

Liz lifted a shoulder. "Special dragons are like characters in a book; I have to go where they want to take me. I have a writer friend who's always saying that."

Lucy let out an excited gasp. "You mean he's a dragon for making up stories?!"

151

"Lucy, don't start," said Liz. "Now, David, if you accept this dragon you must promise to care for him always."

"You mustn't ever make him cry," said Lucy.

David ran a thumb along the dragon's snout. "Erm, this might sound like a silly question, but how is it possible to make him cry?"

"By not loving him," said Lucy, as if it ought to be obvious.

"Imagine that there's a spark inside him," said Liz.

"If you love him, it will always stay lit," smiled Lucy.

"To light it, you must give him a name," said Liz.

"Something magic," said Lucy. "Think of one — now!"

David had a think. "How about . . . Gadzooks?"

Now that Lucy knows Gadzooks is a writing dragon, she asks David to make up a story for her about how Conker damaged his eye. Initially, David refuses. But later, with Gadzooks's help, he begins a tale about

Conker and another squirrel named Snigger, as a present for Lucy on her birthday. This story turns out to be not only a recounting of events that have already occurred, but also a prophetic scribing of the near future. Whatever David writes about, happens.

In time, David and Lucy do manage to catch both Conker and Snigger (the latter accidentally). Along with Liz, they take the two squirrels to the vet at a wildlife hospital, where Sophie, a young woman David likes, works. Snigger is given a clean bill of health, but Conker is not so fortunate. He is given only a short time to live. Hoping to give the dying animal a last few happy days, the group releases the squirrels in the library gardens. David manages to finish his story for Lucy, but the ending is very rushed and unsatisfactory. David is trying to give it a positive outcome, but becomes frustrated and ignores Gadzooks when this seems impossible. Gadzooks becomes very unhappy, to the point where he is in danger of crying his fire tear.

A fire tear is something that a dragon cries at the end of its life. Inside it is all the fire that was within the dragon throughout its existence. This tear then falls off the dragon's snout, drops onto the ground, and finds its way back to the fire at the center of the Earth, from whence it originally came. The only exception to this is related in a legend that runs through *The Fire Within*. This legend concerns Gawain, the last-known real (or "natural") dragon in the world, and after whom one of Lucy's "special" dragons is named.

David yawned and snuggled into his pillow, faintly aware of movement on the bed. It felt lighter, suddenly. More freedom to move. He stretched his legs and cuddled Winston. His body relaxed. His mind drifted. He saw Gawain on a mountaintop, silhouetted against the shimmering moon; Guinevere, wrapped in a kind of shawl, singing into the shell of his ear. Gradually, the dragon lowered his head. His spiked tail drooped. His scales fell flat. His oval eyes, long-closed and weary, blinked one final, fiery time. His life expired in a snort of vapor. But in that moment, a teardrop formed. A living teardrop, on his snout. A violet flame in a dot of water. It trickled down his face to the tip of his nostrils and fell, sparkling, into Guinevere's hands.

But could she survive the power of the dragon's auma? And can David correspondingly save Gadzooks from shedding his own fire tear? What happens when David rewrites the end of Lucy's story? And what has Spikey, the hedgehog, got to do with it all? Well, some things are best revealed by reading the book. . . .

ICEFIRE

The second book in the Last Dragon Chronicles series opens with David receiving the latest in a long line of rejection letters from various publishers. He has been trying repeatedly to get his squirrel story accepted, but with no success so far.

By now, David has discovered that, as a child, Liz was given a mysterious snowball, a pinch of which enables her to bring her clay dragons to life. He is interested to find out the secret of this "icefire," which he knows is guarded by polar bears in the frozen north. When the enigmatic Professor Bergstrom, a visiting academic at the college, tells him about a competition to win a research trip to the High Arctic in Canada, David is desperate to win it. The rules, though, are rather unusual. He must write an essay about whether dragons ever existed on the Earth. David decides to ask Liz for information. At the same time, he begins writing a second book, *White Fire*, about the Arctic and polar bears.

David gets further help for his essay from a Goth girl named Zanna, who is taking the same course as him. She offers to lend him a book on dragons. As his girlfriend, Sophie, is now away working in Africa for eight months, David feels somewhat awkward about inviting Zanna to Wayward Crescent, especially since Liz and Lucy have gone out that afternoon. Nevertheless, he shows Zanna the Dragons' Den. While there, she spies a wishing dragon, G'reth, made by Lucy, and a bronze clay egg. Zanna persuades David to make a wish.

David screwed up his face. "I'm not playing wishing games."

"It's not a game, dummy. You're raising his auma. Believe. *Wish for something — about Gawain."*

"Such as?"

"Such as finding out where his fire tear *is hidden?"*

David stepped back, shaking his head. "No. That's not a good idea." Not here, *he thought,* with all these dragons looking on.

Zanna grabbed him by the sleeve and tugged him forward. "The fact that you're afraid of this only confirms you think it could happen. Do you want to know the truth or not?"

David sighed and looked away. This is ridiculous, *he told himself.* It won't work. It can't work. A wishing dragon? It was the stuff of fairy tales. *But knowing he'd get no peace until he tried, he touched his thumbs to G'reth's smooth paws.*

"Careful," whispered Zanna, "you're making him wobble."

*David steadied his hands and tried again. "I wish," he
whispered, "that I knew the secret of Gawain's fire tear."*

Zanna, meanwhile, who feels oddly drawn to the clay
egg, somehow manages to "kindle," or awaken, it. These
two actions result in an immediate response from the
Universe.

An evil sibyl named Gwilanna turns up, calling herself "Aunty Gwyneth." She claims to be a relation of
Liz and Lucy's. She demands to see Liz, who arrives
home almost at the same moment. Gwilanna has been
"called" by the wisher, and is surprised to detect a
powerful auma change in Liz, denoting that she is the
equivalent of pregnant ("eggnant"?) because of the kin-
dling of the bronze egg by Zanna.

In theory this pregnancy should not be possible.
Gwilanna believes that Liz's auma is getting stronger,
while, with all the other descendants of Guinevere (for
that is what Liz and Lucy are) it is getting weaker,
generation by generation, as expected. "Aunty Gwyneth"
questions why this exception might be so. Getting no

response from either Liz or Lucy on the subject, she determines to interrogate the wishing dragon instead. Gwilanna demands help from Gretel, another Pennykettle dragon, who belongs to her and is under her power.

G'reth gulped and swallowed a plug of smoke. Under normal circumstances, this would not have caused any problems for him. But the fact that he was hanging upside down, tail knotted around a thin wire coat hanger, which in turn was hooked around the lightbulb holder swinging precariously left and right, had brought on a dreadful bout of coughing, which only added to his predicament — and his fear.

Aunty Gwyneth clicked her fingers.

Gretel, sitting on the ledge of the wardrobe, opened her throat and released a jet of fire. There was a smell of burning and the green ground wire in the core of the light cord sizzled red-hot and duly snapped. The cord lurched, jerking G'reth another millimeter or two toward the mass of rubble littering the floorboards. Though his wings were bound (by Aunty Gwyneth's industrial-strength hairpins) he nevertheless managed to swing his head upward. All that remained of the electrical cord now was a strand from the outer sheath of white and the light blue neutral wire. With a whimpering hrrr? *he looked toward Gretel. She blew a tart wisp of smoke and looked away.*

Getting no useful information from G'reth, Gwilanna decides to take a sneakier approach and aid David in his quest to get to the Arctic, hoping that he will discover more on her behalf. To this end she fluences an editor to not only accept David's squirrel book, but also to publish his polar bear saga. Zanna wins the essay competition, but David can now afford to pay his own way for the field trip, using the money due to him for writing his books.

But what about Liz and the egg?

Liz is semi-comatose while the egg is going through the hatching process. The boy that Liz has been told to expect turns out to be a male dragon, the first "natural" dragon to be born in modern times. Zanna reaches out to touch it, and is scarred by Gwilanna's fingernails with three jagged lines which never heal. Under cover of this distraction, the dragon escapes through the open window and, aided by G'reth, flies to Bergstrom's rooms. David, having overcome Gwilanna, follows with Zanna and Gretel. Gretel, by now, has swapped her loyalties to become Zanna's dragon.

At Rutherford House, where Bergstrom lives, Zanna discovers that the young natural dragon, whom she calls Grockle, has been born without fire. She is upset by this, even more so when he turns to stone in her arms, and totally distraught when she finds out that David suspected this might happen, but failed to warn her.

Zanna disappears, refusing to speak to David. Although he tries to find her, he has no luck. The days pass and eventually, just before David is due to go to the Arctic, the contract from the publisher arrives.

"Sign," Lucy urged him.

But Liz raised a hand. "Wait. Have you read through this?"

"Sort of. It's just . . . legalities and stuff."

"Exactly. You ought to know what you're signing. Perhaps Henry could check it for you?"

"It's all right," said David. "It's just boring blurb. Don't spoil my big moment. Pen, someone?"

Lucy grabbed one off the countertop and handed it over.

"Signed . . . David . . . Rain," David muttered, scratching his name on the line marked "author."

David has no time to do anything further — his ride to the airport is about to arrive and he therefore asks Liz to mail the contract to the publisher for him.

Liz picked it up off the kitchen table. For a moment she stood there reading a chunk, then she began to quickly flick through it. At the final page, she stopped and stared. "Lucy, you know that pen, the one David used to sign his name. Does it leak?"

Lucy drew a few lines with it, on her hand. "A bit, yes."

"As much as that?" Liz turned the page around.

From the lower curves of David's signature, three long trails of ink had formed.

Lucy tilted her head . . . and shuddered. "They look like Zanna's scratch."

Was Lucy right to shudder? What effect will these lines called "the mark of Oomara" have on Zanna and on

The mark of Oomara

David? Will David find the secret of Gawain's fire tear, as he wished? And if so, will he live to regret it?

FIRE STAR

David makes it to the field trip, with Zanna by his side again, and continues writing his book. Things are beginning to get more and more complex and confusing for him, though, as he realizes that once again, his writing is mirroring real life. This leads him into questioning his beliefs about the world and his role in it, especially when something called a fire star becomes more and more apparent in the sky, and this portal is due to open a way between worlds.

David has been writing that Gwilanna is determined to raise the natural dragon, Gawain, from a mountaintop on an island in the Arctic called the Tooth of Ragnar. This mountain is where Gawain cried his fire tear and turned to stone in ages past. Guinevere, the woman who caught his tear, had allegedly agreed to trade it with Gwilanna for a daughter. However, the trade never took place.

The child, Gwendolen, was brought up by Gwilanna, but eventually turned her back on the sibyl and went to live among the bears, earning their love and respect. Gwilanna has always hated the bears for this, and is therefore prepared to use them selfishly for her own devious ends.

David writes that Gwilanna has promised to heal a bear named Ingavar, who has been shot, if he will retrieve a certain polar bear tooth for her. David carries this talisman around his neck on a cord. Gwilanna tells Ingavar to kill him when he has succeeded.

David's story finally comes to a head when he and Zanna are faced with Ingavar at a trading post in Chamberlain. Fortunately, Ingavar is tranquilized and taken away to "polar bear prison." The tooth, however, is lost in the melee, but is picked up by Tootega, the Inuit guide who works at the research base where David and Zanna are staying.

Zanna, by now aware that David has the power to write "fact" rather than simply fiction, is none too happy about this state of affairs.

"This is just too spooky," said Zanna. "Read the story, Dr. Bergstrom. Now."

Bergstrom glanced at the open laptop, weaving colored pipework on its flat gray screen.

"No, I'm destroying it," David said. He stepped forward and moved the mouse. Bergstrom immediately clamped his arm.

"You have a contract, remember?"

David looked into the scientist's eyes. It wasn't clear whether Bergstrom was referring to Apple Tree Publishing or the personal promise David had made him to keep on writing about the Arctic. Even so, David said, "I'm wiping it." And he dragged the file into the computer's trash can and emptied it.

This was still not enough for Zanna. "Defrag the disk."

"What?"

"I don't want it in memory, even in bits. Run a defrag over it. Now."

"But — ?"

"Just do it, David."

"Be my guest," said Bergstrom, wheeling his chair away.

Silently furious, David ran the program that would rearrange the disk so all the files were contiguous and any scraps of deleted files were eliminated. "There. Happy now?"

Unbeknown to David, however, Bergstrom has previously printed out a copy — but to what purpose? Anders Bergstrom is definitely not what he first appeared to be. A lecturer, yes, but much, much more than that, for not many professors can shape-shift between man and polar bear ... or possess a small dragon not unlike those that Liz makes, who can Travel through space and time, also shape-shift, and become invisible to boot. . . .

Meanwhile, back at Wayward Crescent, Gwilanna has abducted Lucy to be a "Guinevere clone" to aid in the raising of Gawain. Lucy has been taken to a cave on the Tooth of Ragnar, where she is to be held for the next three months, until the fire star is in its correct alignment. While there, she finds an isoscele, the last scale of a dragon's tail, belonging to Gawain, which she hides from Gwilanna.

After a frantic phone call from Liz, informing him of Lucy's fate, David returns home early from the Arctic. Zanna remains behind and, with Tootega, helps release the tranquilized Ingavar back onto the ice. Gwilanna, in raven form, creates a blizzard, hoping to steal the tooth at last, but her plans backfire when three polar bears arrive and carry Zanna off with them.

While all this is happening, G'reth, the wishing dragon, is still trying to fulfill his duty and find the whereabouts of Gawain's fire tear for David. Rather like David, his investigations are about to take him far beyond what he might have expected. He manages to Travel outside the boundaries of the known Universe and there meets up with a young entity from a race called the Fain.

He had a startling impression of emptiness now. No light. No color. No temperature. No smell. And yet he sensed he was not alone.

He was not.

He felt it enter through the tip of his tail, lift the scales along his spine, and whisper through the tunnels of his spiky ears. Intelligence, finding its level, like water. A youthful, happy being, fusing with his auma.

What are you? *it said, tickling his thoughts.*

What are you? *G'reth asked it.*

I am Fain, *it said.* Shall we commingle?

The Fain are thought-beings who have no physical form of their own, but can merge or "commingle" with any other entity, sharing their host's body. They have a long and benevolent historical connection with dragons, and their ultimate aspiration is to merge with one. G'reth is transformed by this experience, returning back to the known Universe along with the young Fain.

By the time G'reth gets home, Liz has taken Bonnington, the Pennykettles' cat, to the vet. It is not good news. Bonnington is dying. His plight does not appear to be helped by drinking some melted icefire water. There is one beneficial outcome from this sad news, however. Grockle, the young natural dragon who turned to stone at the end of *Icefire*, has been brought back to the Dragons' Den, where he rests in a basket of straw. With the aid of the young Fain being and a drop of Bonnington's saliva, the Pennykettle dragons bring Grockle back to full life. Once again, Grockle escapes through an open window.

David asks Gadzooks for help to find Grockle.

[Gadzooks] scribbled something fiercely across the pad. Gretel and G'reth leaned in to take a look, exchanging a puzzled hrrr *at what they saw. David closed his eyes to picture the message. It surprised him too. A name:*

ARTHUR

THE LIGHT AND THE DARK

He whispered it aloud.

As usual, he had no idea what it meant (at first). Insight would come a little later, from Liz. Right then, however, she was incapable of speech.

She had just fainted in a heap on the floor.

David discovers that Arthur is the love of Liz's life. Many years earlier, he was tricked by Gwilanna into breaking off the relationship and has had no contact with Liz since. Eventually, David traces Arthur to a place called Farlowe Island, where he has become a monk, changing his name to Brother Vincent. Arthur has also been writing fact as fiction, using a claw belonging to Gawain as a pen. Grockle, seeking the claw, has been drawn to the island and hidden there by Arthur. Arthur's secret is given away to the abbot by one of the other monks, Brother Bernard, who later regrets his actions, as Grockle is captured, held in a stable block, and tortured.

Bernard, realizing that what Arthur has told him is

Grockle in chains

the plain truth and that the dragon is sentient and capable of communicating with him, asks:

"Where did you come from?"

The dragon raked the ground. It seemed to understand, but its answer was vague and made no sense.

Zannnnnaaaa, *it growled.*

"Zannnnaaa? What is Zannnnaaa?" Bernard said, frowning.

The dragon swung its head. The chain links rippled in the flashes of daylight streaking through the holes in the derelict roof.

Muuuuutthherrrrr.

The word rumbled around the stable. In a glassless window high in the gable away to their right, the raven landed with a flutter of its wings. A tic developed at Brother Bernard's mouth. "Mother?" he whispered.

The dragon whimpered.

"Then who is your father?"

With another fierce toss of its head, the dragon graarked as though the question was worthy of a bolt of fire. But no fire came. That area of its body still bound by mailing tape bulged with the instinct to spread its wings. But there was no release. Its muted tail pounded the floor in frustration. Its talons raked the earth. It gave no answer.

"Tell me," said Bernard, his throat growing sore from the demands of a language so lacking in vowels.

"Who is your father?"

Caarrkkk! *went the raven, making Bernard jump. This bird was beginning to make him uneasy. There was a dark light in the center of its eye. Why was it so often in attendance to the dragon? Was it some kind of familiar? he wondered. A spirit that served the needs of the creature? He heard footsteps nearby. The raven heard them, too. With another moody* caark, *it circled the barn and swooped back into the open air. Startled voices remarked upon it: Brothers Terence and Peter.*

Bernard centered on the dragon again, "Quickly. Your father?"

The yellow eyes closed. The arches of the nostrils flared like trumpets. Gaaaawwwaaaaaainn, *said his distant descendant, Grockle.*

Bernard backed away with a hand against his throat.

Gawain.

That was all the proof he needed.

Meanwhile, Brother Vincent is locked in his cell, and an off-island envoy sent for, to establish what should be done about the situation.

Unfortunately, when G'reth brought back the young Fain entity to this world, another Fain being came, too. This one was a killer, out to punish G'reth's newfound friend, and to stop the fire star portal between Earth and the home thought-world of the Fain, Ki:mera, from opening. This entity took over the body of the envoy to Farlowe Island, desiring to find Grockle also, and cleanse this world of dragons. However, Grockle starts a fire, reclaims Gawain's claw, and escapes from the island, making his way to the Arctic, the Tooth of Ragnar, and the portal. The evil Fain follows. David is also in hot pursuit, using Bergstrom's invisible dragon, Groyne, to take him there through time and space.

Having reached the Tooth, David finds that Tootega

is already there, but his body has been taken over by the killer Fain being. A dramatic confrontation occurs, with unforeseen results for David and all those connected to him.

Did Grockle make it through the portal in time? Why has Gwilanna been trapped as a raven in an ice block? What will Liz do when she discovers that Arthur's mind was entered by the evil Fain, leaving him terrified, confused, and nearly blind? Did the young Fain escape its evil pursuer? And just what exactly is Bergstrom up to?

THE FIRE ETERNAL

Five years have passed since the end of *Fire Star*. David has been missing in the Arctic for all this time, and is presumed dead by all but Lucy. Despite this, daily life in the Crescent has returned to relative normality for the Pennykettles — and for Zanna, David's long-term partner, and their child, Alexa, who now both live with

THE LIGHT AND THE DARK

Lucy and Liz. Arthur has moved in, too, having been nursed back to relative health by the family. He remains blind.

Alexa is nearly five. A very bright child, she has powers and awarenesses that are only just becoming apparent, and are yet to be taken seriously. On the anniversary of David's disappearance, Zanna presents Alexa with a gift.

"Listen carefully," said Zanna, dropping down on one knee. She brushed a curl of black hair off Alexa's forehead. "You know we talked about polar bears and the icy place they live?"

"Yes," said Alexa, possibly hopeful of receiving one.

Zanna looked at her a moment and tried to frame the words. Those eyes. His eyes. That rich, dark blue. Unsettling and comforting, all in one glance. "Your daddy gave me a dragon there once. I want you to have him, because . . . because Mommy can't take care of him anymore."

The little girl frowned and tilted her head. "Mommy, why are you crying?" she asked.

Zanna bracketed her hands as if she were holding an invisible piece of rock. "You have to look very, very hard to see him. But he's there. He's real. His name is G'lant and his is a flame that will never die out." She opened her hands — as if she were scattering the ashes of her grief — and set G'lant down on Alexa's palms.

The girl looked thoughtfully at the space above her gloves. "I like him," she said.

This gesture seems to set Zanna free of some of her grief, and when a handsome young man named Tam Farrell appears to show an interest in her, she considers responding. Tam, however, is a journalist who has been contacted anonymously by Lucy, who believes it is high time that someone did something about trying to find David. She thinks Tam might be able to help in the search. Tam visits the shop that Zanna owns and buys a ("normal") clay dragon, while casually probing for information about David Rain.

It's not long before the Pennykettle dragons work out that Tam is not quite what he claims to be. Determined to put matters right, they set up a chain of events that result in Tam's girlfriend giving the game away to Zanna just before Tam is due to have a reflexology consultation with her. Zanna, of course, is angry and upset with Lucy, but with Tam especially.

"You know, for one foolish moment, I let myself believe that you could be something special, like David, when all you were giving me were lies and deceit."

"I can help you," he insisted, coughing out pungent, oil-sweet smoke. "If you tell the world the truth, it will only raise your profile even more."

"Truth?" said Lucy. "What do you mean?"

Tam shook his head. "That he never existed. The author of the book: David Rain. He's a cipher. It's all just a front, isn't it?"

In an attempt to prove Tam wrong, Lucy persuades him to take her to the address David wrote on his letter to Liz when responding to her original "room for rent" ad. However, events take a terrifying turn when, having found the place, Lucy is pulled through a rift in space by an evil force. She finds herself on Farlowe Island, among the community of monks who live there. But the monks have been taken over, en masse, by the Ix.

The Ix are the negative version of the benevolent Fain, and use the power of fear to break down any resistance to their plans. They are particularly interested in Lucy because of her ancestry of dragons and her ability to create sculptures, inherited from her mother. They force her to make an antidragon from a compound called obsidian. The template for this creature, which they call a darkling, is generated from a hallucination based on Lucy's deepest dread.

In general shape it resembled a dragon. Serpentine body. Powerful wings. But it was thicker-set and ugly. Cabbage ears. A gargoyle. Its feet and paws were stout and immensely strong, the claws inside them conical, tapering to points. It had no ordered rows of scales. Instead, the surface of its body was pocked and ridged as if the skin had been sheared from brittle rock. And apart from its pulsing, bile-colored eyes, hooked green tongue, and gray-tipped claws, it was completely black. Yet Lucy could see lightning spidering inside it, as though she had opened a box of mirrors. She shook her head in fear as the creature turned toward her. With a granitelike click it unlatched its jaw. From its throat came a bolt of pure black fire.

And when she has done that, they intend to send her back through the same time rift they took her from but commingled with an Ix assassin. . . .

In the meantime, David has found out a lot more about who and what he is, his history, and his purpose on the planet. We also learn where he has been and what has happened to him in the past five years.

David is now in the Arctic, attempting to save his beloved polar bears — and indeed the world. He has teamed up with two of them, Kailar and Avrel, to search for the opening to the Fire Eternal, the most creative force in the Universe. David has in his possession the stone eye of Gawain, which has been brought up from the ocean depths by the sea goddess, Sedna. David intends to open the eye and free the spirit of the dormant dragon at last.

David is also accompanied by Gwilanna, who was left as a raven and trapped in a block of ice at the end of the previous book. Despite being a nuisance, Gwilanna agrees to help David with his quest, on the promise of being returned to human form by the end of it.

However, events take a surprising turn when an ancient mammoth appears in front of them all.

David is quick to recognize it as a projection sent by his daughter, Alexa, as a token of her love. However, Kailar is hexed into perceiving it as something else.

Kailar gave out a fighting growl and immediately drew up parallel to the mammoth's flank. Ignoring Ingavar's previous instruction, he began pacing back and forth in a threatening manner, his head held low, his black tongue issuing from the side of his mouth. It was a gibe to the creature to come and challenge him.

Avrel tightened his claws. There was going to be trouble.

Indeed there was.

David urgently sends Gwilanna back to Wayward Crescent to protect Alexa when he realizes that his daughter's auma trail must have been detected by the Ix, via the projection she sent. Gwilanna returns just in time to face the Ix:risor, or assassin, that is Lucy. There are devastating and far-reaching effects as a result of the confrontation, some of which echo throughout the rest of the series.

David, meanwhile, is nearing the end of his quest, and polar bears in their hundreds are gathering around the gateway to the Fire Eternal. . . .

What does David intend to do with all the congregated bears? Can he open Gawain's eye? Who does Lucy try to kill? And does she succeed? Which

Pennykettle dragon is in dire danger of extinction? And why is an ornamental "fairy door" so important? Will David ever return to Wayward Crescent?

DARK FIRE

The fifth book in the series is the darkest of them all. It deals with (obviously!) dark fire, the most destructive force in the Universe.

The weather has gone completely weird; there is a mist over the Arctic that nothing can penetrate, and natural dragons are back to recolonize the Earth. As if all this worldwide hoo-ha wasn't enough to be getting on with, things are not so straightforward back in leafy suburbia either. . . .

David Rain appears unannounced one day in the Pennykettles' kitchen, where Zanna finds him sitting calmly at the table, apparently unconcerned about the upset his disappearance, and subsequent reappearance, has caused.

"Five years you were gone."

"I didn't know that."

"Five Christmases, five birthdays, five Father's Days, five . . . Valentine's." Five letters, she was thinking bitterly, remembering how she'd always written one to him on that day in mid-February, the anniversary of his apparent "death." *"And then you just turn up out of nowhere?"*

"I couldn't help it," he repeated. *"The Fain took me back. Into the world they call Ki:mera, a place where time is meaningless."*

"Not to me." She forced her pretty face forward. *"Just go, David. Disappear into your weird Fain world. Leave me alone to look after my child."*

Zanna is doubly upset as she has just discovered a strange rash on Alexa's back while bathing her. The little girl doesn't seem to be troubled by it, but it is yet one more thing to add to the growing list of anxieties that pervade the Pennykettle household.

Liz is pregnant again, this time naturally, and Lucy is not her old self at all. Although the Ix assassin within her has gone, she is still feeling guilty and in shock about what it made her do. As if all this wasn't enough, Henry, the Pennykettles' cranky next-door neighbor, is ill, and his sister, Agatha, arrives to look after him. Agatha turns out to be another sibyl, one of many that seem to be popping up all over the world as the twelve natural dragons from the old Wearle, or colony, are being awakened from their prolonged sleep.

The whereabouts of these dragons' resting places is becoming the subject of intense interest since Arthur received a phone call from an old friend, Rupert Steiner. Rupert has been visited by a small dragon, later identified as Gadzooks, who has left a message on a piece of Steiner's best notepaper.

Arthur, with Liz and Lucy (and Lucy's special dragon, Gwendolen — along for the ride as a GPS) go to see Rupert at his home in Cambridge. There, with Gwendolen's help, they discover that Gadzooks had written the word "Scuffenbury" — but in dragontongue.

Steiner recalls that he has seen some similar marks in some photographs he was once sent, taken in a cave at a place called the Hella glacier, in the Arctic. Using Gadzooks's message as a key, he ultimately manages to decipher the writings on the wall of the cave. They turn out to be the record of a meeting between the last twelve dragons in the world (the Last Dragon Chronicles, in fact). The writings are subsequently published by Tam in his newspaper's magazine.

Lucy is thoroughly thrown by what she learns from this article. It becomes obvious that one of these twelve dragons is lying dormant at Scuffenbury, beneath a hill called Glissington Tor. David persuades Lucy to go there with Tam.

"I've booked us in here."

"The Old Gray Dragon?"

"It's a guesthouse," he said. "Bed-and-breakfast. Right on the side of the Tor. It says in their blurb that on a still night you can hear the dragon snoring. I thought it might make you feel at home."

But "at home" is the last thing that Lucy feels. A terrifying nightmare while asleep on the first night is followed by a series of further nightmares in broad daylight. The owners of the guest house, Hannah and Clive, *seem* like perfectly pleasant people; the only other guest, a Ms. Gee, while a little eccentric and "standoffish" *appears* to want nothing more than to be left alone; and as for *the cat* — well, the guesthouse owners deny any knowledge of a cat. . . .

It all starts off innocently enough with Tam and Lucy deciding to take a walk up the hill opposite the Tor, to survey the land. Lucy, looking across the valley, spots something out of the ordinary.

"I think there's someone on the Tor."

His footsteps halted. She saw him squint in that scary polar bear fashion, just the way David sometimes did. "Probably a tourist. People come here all the time." He started along the path again, almost bounding where it hollowed out into a dip.

Lucy scrabbled after him, glancing at the figure every now and then. Comparatively speaking it was nothing but a matchstick, but Lucy, blessed with the eyesight of youth, could still work out its basic movements. She saw the arms come parallel with the shoulders. Half-stretched, not full, as if the person might be cupping their hands above their eyes. Or holding a pair of binoculars.

But things deteriorate rapidly from there, especially once they discover that the person watching them is yet another sibyl.

And speaking of sibyls, Gwilanna has gone missing, along with the isoscele of Gawain and an obsidian knife, which she had stolen from the Ix that had invaded Lucy. David is eager to find Gwilanna, not only because she is highly dangerous in her own right, but also because the knife contains a spark of dark fire. The leader of the new Wearle, a natural dragon called G'Oreal, gives David the task of recovering the dark fire, which is then to be taken north to be destroyed.

David solicits Zanna's help in locating Gwilanna, and Zanna obliges by tracking and following the sibyl to Farlowe Island. Once there, Zanna finds she has walked into a trap. Gwilanna is in a maudlin mood, lamenting the fact that she should have been granted illumination (a spiritual merging) with the offspring of a dragon called Ghislaine, but was cheated out of it. Gwilanna has created a force field around the circle of standing stones in the middle of the island, within which Zanna, and the dark fire, are held.

"The circle will magnify the spark behind you and the Fain will see it from here to Ki:mera. By the time they arrive, I will be gone — with the obsidian — and my terms will be written in your blood across the stones: Give me illumination — or I take the dark fire to the Ix."

But Gwilanna's plans go awry, and the spell that was intended to put the specter of the dragon Ghislaine to rest instead attracts the auma of a very different — and terrifying — creature. A flock of ravens roosting nearby are also affected by the energy flow and begin to mutate . . . with far-reaching consequences.

These raven-mutants cause mayhem and destruction wherever they go. But in the initial confusion at the stone circle, the one saving grace is that Gwilanna, although still free, has been forced to leave the dark fire behind. This Zanna gives to David, who retains it for his own purposes, rather than take it north to the Wearle, as directed. But possession of the dark fire brings interest from the Ix. Zanna is concerned that the Ix are too much of a threat in a general sense, and is worried for the family's safety specifically. David decides to tell her more about the situation.

"[Y]ou're right, the Ix can't be defeated as such — but their negative auma can be transmuted."

"Oh, yeah? Tell that to Lucy. She's still scared out of her wits by them."

"I have talked to Lucy," he said. His gaze drifted sideways, compressing into bitterness. "She was attacked by an Ix:risor, a highly intensified Ix grouping, sometimes

called a Comm:Ix or a Cluster. When they're concen-
trated into a conglomerate like that they become almost
impossible for the human mind to resist. But that's
exactly the state we need them in: one huge cluster. It's
getting them there that's the difficult part."

"And whose finger will be on the trigger when you
do? I'd never seen that mangy crone Gwilanna scared
until she talked about you meddling with the Fire
Eternal."

"It won't be me," he said, and looked at her hard.

Slowly, the implication in his gaze began to register.
"No," she said, covering the scars on her arm. "If you
put Alexa in any kind of danger, I'll —"

"Alexa is already in danger," he said, with a calm-
ness she found unsettling. To her deeper dismay, she
realized she was trying hard not to cry.

The danger for the whole family continues to increase.
Even Sophie (David's first girlfriend) e-mails from
Africa to say that she thinks something is amiss with

her "special" dragon, Grace. The tension builds; breaking point is imminent.

Back at Scuffenbury, Lucy succeeds in awakening the dormant dragon there, but with drastic effect and at great cost to herself and those around her. Tam is missing, several others are dead, and although David sends Grockle to help her, she finds that that help may be too little and too late.

When she looked again, Glissington Tor had broken into four distinct mounds, and rising from its smoking center was the most terrifying dragon she had ever seen.

It was green, savage, and at least three times the size of Grockle. When it threw out its wings it blocked the sun and seemed to draw the landscape around it like a blanket. From nostril to tail it must have measured half a small field. For a moment or two it kept its head folded into its chest, but when it raised its snout and Lucy saw the redness in one eye, the bones at the base of her spine turned to jelly. The dragon had been horribly attacked at some time. Or maybe something had failed with its fire tear? Or the eye had become diseased in some way? She couldn't tell. Nor could she bear to look at it for long. But little did she know she would soon be forced to. For just as the unicorn had sensed her presence, suddenly the dragon seemed to scent her as well. The scales around its neck came up in a frill and black smoke gushed from its long, narrow snout. Paying no heed whatsoever to Grockle, it turned its damaged gaze on Lucy. At first she told herself it couldn't have seen her. She had to be a mile and a half away, at least. But with a wallop of wings that tickled the blades of grass around her feet, the thing took off and headed their way. In mid-flight, it uncoupled its jaw and let out a squeal that sounded like a pig being forced through a grinder. Lucy saw Grockle tense. The squeal gathered force and grew into a roar, which seemed loud enough to shatter the dome of the sky. Lucy covered her ears and screamed.

Lucy meets her destiny

The arrival on the scene of darklings and hordes of Ix entities intensifies the situation even further and a full-scale battle commences in the skies over Scuffenbury.

Dun-dun-dunnnn . . . You know what to do to find out whether Lucy — or any of the other characters — survive or not. What happens to Liz's child — if indeed it is a child? What fate has Gwilanna brought upon herself?

What is the new species that is to be introduced into the world, according to David? Will Mother Earth herself turn against its human occupants if the Ix win the battle and an inversion occurs? Will the light of the world turn finally to an eternal dark . . . ?

FIRE WORLD

Without giving too much away, the dramatic conclusion to the battle at Scuffenbury Hill sees the story take a sideways step into another dimension — literally.

Co:pern:ica, the "Fire World" of the title, is an experimental world created by the Fain using templates of humans from Earth. Thus, the people of Earth have counterparts on Co:pern:ica, "constructs" who are similar but not identical to themselves. The Co:pern:ican versions may differ by name or relationship, but have largely similar roles to play in their respective lives. All the regular characters from the first five books are here, but not as you've known them before. For example, Anders Bergstrom, on Earth a mentor to David Rain, becomes Thorren Strømberg, a psychological counselor to David Merriman. The people who inhabit Co:pern:ica have the ability to "imagineer" — to materialize objects from thought and intention alone. The idea behind the manifestation of this world was to create a society whereby everyone had access to all they needed, within certain limits set by the Higher (as the Fain are collectively known on Co:pern:ica).

Problems first occur when David, then twelve years old, begins to imagineer outside the Grand Design. This becomes apparent during his sleep cycles, when he has nighttime disturbances so severe that he is taken by his parents, Eliza and Harlan, to see Counselor

Strømberg, who films him while asleep. The film reveals a surprising and frightening development.

For the first few frames, David lay on his back with his hands tucked under his therma:sol sheet. Then, just as if a pin had been stuck into his foot, his head twitched away from the camera and came violently back, making an audible whack *against his pillow. He drew up his knees. His back arched slightly. His hands began to push the sheet away.*

Suddenly, the screen flashed as if a light had popped. At the same time, David jerked up in bed with his jaws wide open and his lips curled back. Two of his teeth seemed slightly extended. His eyes, normally so placid and round, slanted sideward and briefly changed color from their usual deep blue to a strong shade of brown. With both hands he clawed wildly at the space in front of him, though nothing appeared to be occupying that space. And out of his throat came an uncommon noise. A roar, not unlike the sound of an engine.

On replaying the film at a slower speed, it becomes evident that David (morphed into a polar bear) was fighting something. Even more strangely, firebirds, the only creatures other than katts on Co:pern:ica, were involved in allaying the danger.

This time, as the colors slipped through the blinds, it was possible to see them re-expand into the familiar long-tailed shapes of the creatures that inhabited every part of Co:pern:ica. Firebirds. Four of them. Green, cream colored, sky blue, and red. They flew to David's bed and hovered in the region of his flashing hands. It was then that Harlan witnessed something even more extraordinary. Just in front of David, over an area approximately two feet long, the air was rippling in a vertical line, as if the fabric of the universe was being torn apart.

"In the name of Co:pern:ica, what's that?" Harlan muttered, and watched in fascination as the firebirds went about sealing the rift with bursts of the white-colored fire that was sometimes seen to issue from their

nostrils. When it was done, they went back the way they'd come. . . .

Harlan buried his hands inside his pockets and let his worried gaze drift back to the screen. The image of David remained there for a moment before Strømberg hit a button and cleared it. "He could be a danger to us all," he said.

So how could a young boy morph into a polar bear? And what was he fighting? Counselor Strømberg asks David's father, who is a scientist, a Professor of Realism, to investigate. Harlan subsequently discovers that the rift is a portal to another dimension, but within the same time frame. The disturbing conclusion from this is that something from another world has tried to contact David. . . .

Thus, for his own safety, it is decreed that David be taken to Bushley librarium, to help calm him down. The librarium is a huge museum of books, and the largest firebird aerie on Co:pern:ica.

It rose out of the flowers like a great gray monolith. A single tall building with an uncountable number of floors. The upper floors were lost in wisps of cloud and the whole structure seemed to be bending backward as though it had reached a critical mass and was ready to topple over at any moment. Fine red sand (or something like it) was raining down from the joints in the brickwork and being taken away in skirts on the breeze. At ground level there was just one door. It was made of wood (unusually) and was twice Harlan's height. It was already halfway open, despite the fact that a small sign badly attached to the door frame invited visitors to R NG THE BE L. *Harlan moved forward to do just that and stepped on something that had spilled out of the doorway. It was a large-format book. He reached down and picked it up. It must have been thirty spins since he'd seen one. He smoothed a film of the red sand off the glossy cover and handed it to Eliza.*

"The Art of Baking Cakes," *she read.*

Harlan shrugged. "Welcome to the librarium."

Eliza opened the pages and looked at several of the ancient digi:grafs. "Why do we keep this stuff? I could easily imagineer anything in this. I don't understand what use this is to anyone."

"Historical value," Harlan said. He took the book from her and flipped through its pages. He showed a digi:graf of a chocolate gateau to David. The boy's eyes lit up and he quickly imagineered a miniature version. He gave it to his mother.

Eliza smiled and de:constructed it. "Bad for your purity of vision," she said.

"I think books are rather quaint," said Harlan. "And they're real, of course, not constructs." He closed the book and laid it back in the doorway. "Our ancestors would have relied on these things."

Eliza shook her head and looked up at the building. "Is this real, do you think?"

Harlan touched the brickwork, feeling its roughness, though that in itself was no proof of authenticity; anyone on Co:pern:ica could imagineer a brick. "Yes," *he said. "I'd be surprised if anyone had enough in their fain to put up something as large as this and still be able to maintain it."*

Eliza sighed and put her hands on David's shoulders, pulling him back toward her a little. "Why would Strømberg send him to a relic like this?"

"Well, let's begin the process of finding out." This time, Harlan did press the bell.

To their surprise, the bell is answered by a girl named Rosa, who quickly becomes David's best friend. Rosa is his age and the assistant of Mr. Henry, curator of the librarium. Her job, and now David's, too, is to put the books into order, both by subject matter and alphabetically. This sounds a thankless — and deadly boring — task, but David soon finds out that books are not only fascinating things for all the information and entertainment they can provide, but also that these particular books, along with the building itself, are alive and filled with auma — energy. The only small niggle in David's and Rosa's idyllic lives is that they can never find a way to get beyond Floor 42, into the levels where they know the firebirds live.

All continues well until Harlan, while trying to recreate the rift in his lab, inadvertently causes a time-jolt and he and everyone connected with him ages eight years, instantly.

For this "crime" he and his assistant, Bernard Brotherton, are banished to the Dead Lands, a huge area of abandoned wasteland beyond Co:pern:ica Central's city limits. Here, they find that isolated pockets of survivors are scratching out an existence for themselves, and the two men are sheltered by one such group, calling themselves Followers of Agawin, a mythical man-dragon of legend. Near to the group's camp is a hill called the Isle of Alavon (it used to be surrounded by water). On the peak of this hill is a tower. Legend has it that the tower was the home of Agawin and is protected by a wraith. Harlan decides to investigate. Along with Bernard and two other men from the group, they reach the tower and find a large stone dais inside it. . . .

Suddenly, Mathew Lefarr cried out: "Harlan, look up!"

There, in the circle of light above, was the apparition they had all imagined but never made flesh. A terrifying beast with wings like giant sheets of canvas. Eyes of yellow oil. Teeth like daggered rocks. It twisted and hissed and roared at the men, all the while lashing its dark red tongue. . . . The creature twisted its ingenious neck (every scale readjusted in one flowing arrow) and aimed its snout downward. Squeezing its nostrils tight, it sent forth a column of blue-white fire. The point of the flame struck the center of the dais. It burned for a sec in a crown of light, then was sucked back into the nostrils of the dragon. In its wake, something extraordinary followed. There was a grinding noise at the center of the dais, and the spot marked by the image of Agawin began to turn and work its way upward. At first it appeared that a plug of pure stone had lifted from the structure. But as Harlan's eyes readjusted to the light, he saw that it was a receptacle of sorts. A cylinder, about the length of a man's hand, made of a glistening, trans:lucent matter. With cinders in his hair and uncomfortable traces of singeing in his nostrils, he took a breath and closed his hand around it. The outer structure vanished as if it were dust, but when he pulled his hand away, inside it was something from another world.

Lefarr was too awestruck to speak at first. "What is it?" he asked eventually.

Harlan ran his thumb along the curved and jagged surface. "Something beyond our reality," he whispered. "I believe it's the claw of a dragon."

Meanwhile, back in Bushley, David, hearing of his father's arrest, has gone back home. To make matters worse for Rosa, two unethical "Aunts" named Primrose and Petunia, representatives of the powers-that-be on Co:pern:ica, arrive at the librarium. Under the orders of the Aunt Su:perior, Gwyneth (Gwilanna by any other name — oh, dear . . .), they attempt to steal the auma from the books to boost their powers of imagineering. Rosa finds the machine they are using to do this:

It was a thin flat pad, about half the size of a standard book cover. It had a sleek black screen, which appeared to have a number of thumbprints on its surface. Flashing lights were jumping back and forth across the bottom, as if the device were waiting for an input. Rosa had never troubled herself with elec:tronics and hadn't sent a single :com in her life. Even so, she picked up the pad and pressed her finger to a likely area of the screen. It lit up at once. A message invited her to SCAN OBJECT. *She looked at Aurielle. The firebird frowned.* Object? *thought Rosa.* What object? *And then it struck her: the books, of course. She picked one off the bed and slowly brought it into contact with the pad. To her horror, the pad came alive. Numbers. Lights. Menus. Colors.*

The machine asks Rosa whether she wants it to absorb the collected energy, but instead she hurls the pad across the room and runs to the nearest shelf of books. She pulls one down and opens it —

For one moment nothing happened. But as she tilted the book, the periods, the commas, the question marks, and eventually the words themselves all began to slip from their places on the page until they were falling like ash around her feet.

"No," she wailed. She sank to her knees, clutching the book to her heart.

They were dead, all of them. She knew it at once. Their auma taken. Their power destroyed. . . .

Rosa looked tearfully over her shoulder. The Aunts were waking. She narrowed her gaze.

Good.

A tussle follows and the machine accidentally disgorges its auma into a strange three-lined scratch on Rosa's arm. Not only can Rosa now read dragontongue, the language in which the mysterious *Book of Agawin* is written (maybe Agawin is not just a legend, after all?), but she can also understand the firebirds when they communicate. Invited onto the upper floors by them, she and David discover an egg (which looks as

Tapestry of Isenfier

if it is ready to hatch) and a tapestry allegedly made by Agawin. They get a huge surprise when they discover that they (or rather, their Earth counterparts) are among a group of people depicted on the tapestry, along with a small dragon, holding a pad and pencil. . . . This is Gadzooks, of course, as you will know if you have read *Dark Fire*. The tapestry shows a scene from the

Battle of Isenfier, a vision from Agawin's distant future. Eventually, David and Harlan discover that Gadzooks has stopped the battle by suspending time and that a beacon or distress call is being sent out across the universe — to them.

Meanwhile, by her usual devious means, Aunt Gwyneth has gotten hold of the dragon's claw which Harlan found in the Dead Lands. Taking the form of a katt so that she can enter the librarium undetected, she commingles with a firebird infected by the Ix and learns it was they who came through the rift in search of David.

We will answer your questions, *they said weakly.*

"Very wise. Tell me more about David Merriman. How can he have the auma of a dragon when no such thing exists on this world?"

The Ix paused. He is between worlds, *they said.*

"There are three *Davids?"*

Negative, *said the Ix.* There is one entity, varying at quantum speeds between the time points. His auma alternates across the planes. This is a primary condition of the nexus.

"Is his life on Earth different — when he's there?"

Yes, but his purpose remains the same. Only the connections vary.

"Connections? What connections?"

The Ix took a moment to consider this question. The mammal in the book is one.

"The squirrel? Why would an insignificant creature mean so much to someone like him?"

On Earth, he has resonated strongly with them. We do not know what their function is.

"And where do I, Gwyneth, fit into this?"

You are another connection.

Suddenly, the tic around the eye was back. "Are you telling me that I have another life — on Earth?"

We must Cluster to answer that.

"Do it," she snapped, flashing the katt's tail. *"Try anything and I'll neutralize you all."*

We accept this, *said the Ix.*

She let them regroup. After several moments of neu-
ral activity, they reported they had an answer.

"Well? What is it?"

At the time of Isenfier, Gwyneth does not exist.

"What?" The katt's teeth began to chatter fiercely.

On Earth, you are called Gwilanna. You die before
Isenfier begins.

"How? In what circumstances?"

Fear, *they said, buzzing around her brain.* Fear of
the Shadow. Fear of the Ix.

Gwyneth instantly decides she must change the timeline
so that "she" does not die after all. But by doing that,
she will change not only her own life on Earth, but also
those of everyone else in the tapestry.

Will she succeed? Who or what can stop her? Will
Gadzooks's message be picked up? And who is the young
boy who has suddenly appeared in the tapestry? — and
what hatches out in the aerie? It certainly doesn't seem
to be a firebird. . . .

212

THE FIRE ASCENDING

The seventh and last book in the series follows what happens when Gwilanna dramatically attempts to save herself by altering the Earth's natural timeline. Her actions cause ripples back through history, enough to change history itself, including the legend of Gawain.

The Fire Ascending begins on Earth, in the era when the last twelve dragons decide to give up their conflict with humans and isolate themselves on mountaintops all around the world. One of them, Galen, comes to land in an area called Kasgerden. This is observed by a young goatherd called Agawin, who is apprentice to a seer named Yolen.

It is traditional that a pilgrimage takes place to honor and pay last respects to a dying dragon, in hope that sparks of its fire tear (known as fraas) may be spread around and bring benefit and healing to any who experience its energy. However, Agawin's excitement at taking part in this event is disrupted by an unexpected commotion.

Those at the rear began crying out a warning. I looked back and saw people stumbling and falling, children being picked up and rushed aside. The ground rumbled to the sound of galloping hooves. Horses were upon us. Arriving at high speed. The crowd parted like a flock of startled birds and I saw an old man knocked brutally sideways by the leading horse. It was as black as the unlit cave, with a mane that flashed around its neck like a blaze. Its eyes were full of blood and anguish. In the center of its forehead, at the level of the eyes, I thought I saw a stump of twisted rock, rough hewn at its point and oozing a kind of syrupy fluid. But my gaze was mostly on the rider, not his mount. Astride the horse sat a thumping brute of a man, with hair as long as the children of Horste. The menace in his eyes was as dark as the fists that gripped the black reins. And though I had no reason then to be afraid of him, a fateful chill still entered my heart.

For even I, a boy of twelve, could tell he was mesmer-ized by the prospect of the dragon. He was hunting more than fraas, I was sure.

The rider of the violated black unicorn turns out to be a man named Voss, who, with his men, mounts a fur-ther attack on the pilgrims. He wishes to kill Galen and take control of the whole area, although he himself is controlled by the Ix. In league with Hilde, the local sibyl, he uses the broken-off portion of the unicorn's horn as a means of gaining and wielding power.

Agawin and Yolen are invited to take refuge with a local villager, Rune, and his family. Rune's daughter, Grella, sees visions of dragons, and makes them into tap-estries, at which she excels. When Agawin is invited to try his hand at starting a tapestry picture, he finds himself drawing a small dragon holding a notepad. He has no idea that this is Gadzooks or what the significance of his drawing might be. Meanwhile, the men of the village are invited to a meeting to decide what to do about Voss, and Agawin takes a walk. He stumbles across a tumbledown dwelling, wherein sits an old man. This is Brunne, a blind seer, who seems to recognize Agawin's importance and tells the boy that he needs to know the secrets of time. Brunne is about to explain further when . . .

He swiftly raised a hand and some force pushed me back into the shadows of the krofft. He gave out a groaning sound like nothing I had heard from man or beast before — a rasp that rattled every bone in his chest, followed by a shudder that seemed to expel something more than air from his lungs. I gasped and covered my face. Whatever Brunne had concealed within his body was now in mine and sheltering there. The last thing I heard him say to me was this: "Keep Galen within your sight."

Within seconds of this transfer, Brunne is murdered by one of Voss's men, and the building is set alight. In the meantime, Agawin hurries back to Rune's krofft. He finds the men drugged and learns that Grella has been taken by Hilde to Voss's campsite on Mount Kasgerden. He follows, with the intention of rescuing Grella, but walks into a trap and is captured himself. Strangely, Voss is in possession of Agawin's tapestry — which now has a young girl pictured in it, a figure that Agawin did not draw. It later transpires that the tapestry is being imagineered by Agawin's own memories and future visions. But who is the child in the picture, and what is she trying to tell Agawin before he is sent hurtling off the mountain by one of Voss's henchmen . . . ? Amazingly, Agawin survives the fall and to his surprise reappears in a distant valley, in front of a striking young woman who introduces herself as none other than Guinevere — the girl who, in legend, will catch Gawain's fire tear.

Guinevere takes Agawin back to the cave where she lives with a local sibyl — Gwilanna. Each is immediately suspicious of the other. Agawin learns that the sibyl was brought up by Grella (whom Gwilanna falsely believes to be her mother), but Gwilanna will not talk about her. Similarly, Gwilanna distrusts Agawin because Grella always told her he had died in his fall. During a tense dialogue, Guinevere rushes into the cave to say that an eagle has appeared carrying an egg between its claws. The eagle is Gideon, and the dragon, about to hatch, is none other than Gawain.

Once he is out of his egg, Gwilanna is not thrilled by the new arrival, even though he is the last-known dragon in the world.

Gawain threw out his wings and went hrrr! *in her face.*

A gobbet of spittle landed on her cheek and fizzed along one of her many wrinkles. "Little monster!" she squealed, pulling back. She rubbed her face dry and swept toward the cave. "Bring that inside. Put it by the fire. When the sun goes down it will need more warmth than you *can give it."*

I looked down at Gawain. He was indeed shivering. But it would not be long before his scales began to show, before he would get the insulation he needed. Dragons grew fast, if I remembered Yolen's teachings correctly. He might look surprisingly vulnerable now, covered in juvenile pimply skin, but in just a few days he would be battle-hardened. "Plated" was the term the old ones used.

So I did as Gwilanna instructed. I went inside and set him by the fire. Right away, he scented the stewing rabbit and leaped into the pot, devouring every chunk, using his tail to skewer pieces up. To Gwilanna's annoyance, he lapped up all the juices as well. Then he licked his feet and isoscele clean and settled in the pot with his tail curled around him, unconcerned by the heat from the flames.

Gwilanna decides that Agawin and Guinevere must leave with the dragon because it would attract too much attention and bring danger to them all. She sends them to an island along the coast, where they believe Gawain will be protected by a nearby tribe called the Inook. Not long into their journey, however, they come upon two unusual riders, a man and a woman, dressed like no one they have ever met before. The woman is riding a white unicorn; the man, a horse. It soon becomes clear that Gawain recognizes the man, and he rushes out of hiding to greet him. After a tense encounter, the man identifies himself as none other than David Rain. His companion is Rosa, Zanna's "alternate" from Co:pern:ica.

David reveals that they have stepped through a fire star on Co:pern:ica, in response to a distress call sent out by Gadzooks. They are here, he says, to seek out Gwilanna. When Guinevere asks why, David explains that in the future, Gwilanna has learned to Travel through time, creating havoc. He goes on to say that the fire star has brought them to early Earth so that they might discover how Gwilanna has gained this ability, and hence find a way to stop her. Agawin pledges his allegiance to the quest and swears he will do all he can to aid them. But Gwilanna, as always, proves to be a difficult and cunning adversary. Before long, she has concocted a plan to abduct Agawin and take him back to Mount Kasgerden. There, using one of Gawain's

claws, she rewrites the timeline in her own favor, and
sends Agawin over the cliff edge again. . . .

I fell and I fell, with no tornaq to protect me. But my
life did not end at the foot of the mountain. It simply
took a different course again. Gwilanna's dishonest use
of the claw had sent signals rippling through the fab-
ric of the universe, signals that Traveled infinitely faster
than a seer's apprentice could chance to fall. As the
darkling rushed away from my sight, three other crea-
tures filled the space around me. Firebirds. One green,
one red, one a beautiful cream color with apricot
flashes around her ear tufts. It was she who spoke to
my consciousness saying, Agawin, we are monitors of
time and the agents of Gideon. Do not be afraid. Joseph
Henry is with you.

Joseph Henry? *I asked. My voice had the texture of*
thickened mud.

But all the firebird said was this: You have been
chosen for illumination. You will die and live again,

through the auma of Gawain. All you have to do is give yourself up to it.

I do not want to die. *Panic gripped my heart.*

It is a change, *she said.* Simply a change.

I was floating now, less aware of my body. All around me, the tiniest stars were glittering. I felt that if I let my consciousness touch one, I would instantly pop into another life. What of Galen?

He will always be with you. In your new form, he will not hinder your progress.

What is the new form?

A hybrid of human, dragon, and Fain.

But that is what I am now.

This time, the energies will be fully commingled. You will go back, to observe Gwilanna. Joseph Henry himself has decreed this. You will be hidden from the sibyl — but always within her sight.

How? How is that possible?

Choose a [fire] star, *the firebird said.* There are many probabilities. Let your instinct guide you.

So I reached out in search of a different life. And in

a timescale I could not measure or estimate, I found the star that was right for me, at a point on the time-line of huge significance, located at a place called Wayward Crescent. I chose, for my dominant form, to be human. And I chose to be born to a very special mother, one who had cause to be close to Gwilanna. The last thing I remembered before I touched my mother's star was the memory of the child I had seen on the tapestry. And at last I understood her purpose and her words. Sometimes we will be Agawin, *she had said. . . .*

From here begins the most unusual twist in the entire series. The fire star Agawin touches, the mother he chooses to be reborn to, is none other than Zanna. In his new life, far along the timeline, he becomes Alexa Martindale. Little wonder, then, that Alexa has always been thought of as "special"!

But what of the quest to stop Gwilanna?

Not surprisingly, the sibyl's irresponsible meddling causes even more chaos. The timeline alters dramatically again. In this version of it, Voss survives and raises a darkling army. The battle at Scuffenbury Hill, suspended in time at the end of *Dark Fire*, begins again but swings in favor of the Ix. The Earth is gripped by the Ix "Shadow," a negative force that sucks color out of vegetation and turns humans and animals alike into ugly "inversions" of themselves, lacking any soul or desire for independence.

The blue planet seems doomed.

But there is one character who is not at all fazed, for he has been carefully engineering some of this, knowing that *sometimes* the only way to prevent evil flourishing is to let it believe it has won. That character is Joseph Henry, Elizabeth Pennykettle's unborn son. Joseph was at the battle of Scuffenbury Hill (in the guise of Gwillan, a Pennykettle dragon), but was cleverly released from it by Gadzooks when the battle was stopped. Free to roam the Universe thereafter, Joseph has studied every possible timeline and found the only course of events that assures victory for David.

Not that it seems straightforward when he explains it to Alexa during a meeting in the librarium on Co:pern:ica.

"Isenfier is upon us," said Joseph. "You must return to the Crescent, where you will be safe." He stood up and made a firebird call. Gideon and the three that had saved me at Kasgerden came flying down from the upper floors.

"Joseph, wait. You never did tell me what happened to Elizabeth."

"Just stay in the Crescent. For my sake now."

"But I vowed to stop Gwilanna."

"You can't," he said. "Only Gwilanna herself can do that."

I spread my wings with a determined phut! *"I have a duty to Galen and the last twelve dragons. Let me be Agawin. Let me* fight."

"What makes you think there will be a fight?"

No fight? *"Then what is your plan?"*

"Gwilanna has set the conditions for Isenfier. Everything now depends on her. We will give her what she craves and let the timeline adjust. It begins the second after she takes you from the woods."

Back in the dawn of history. With Gawain.

"Your book will record it all," he said. He nodded at the lectern where the book was waiting.

But my mind was still hovering firmly on Gwilanna. "Give her what she craves?"

He signaled to Gadzooks. The dragon lifted his pencil.

And as I felt the strange tug of the universe turning, I watched Joseph Henry fade away and commingle with the body of the firebird Gideon. "We need to give her what she's always wanted, Agawin." He spread his brown wings and snorted fire from his nostrils. "Illumination to a dragon."

And that is exactly what happens. Gwilanna becomes illumined to Gawain himself. David and Rosa are captured by Voss's army and brought before the "inverted" dragon. Who in this dreadful dark world can save them? Well, Joseph Henry and Alexa are far from defeated. Nor are the polar bears that disappeared at the end of *Dark Fire*. And there is one other group of characters that should never be underestimated by the most evil of warlords. Here are some clues to their identity: They're green, spiky, made of clay, have large flat feet and trumpet-shaped nostrils, and usually announce themselves with a little *hrrr*. . . .

This chapter has been a very swift run-through of some of the funny and some of the exciting story lines. As with all the other books in the series, there are many more plots that I have deliberately barely mentioned, or not even touched on, in *The Fire Ascending*. That leaves a lot for you to discover and to enjoy for yourself. Look out in particular for a gruesome story from Gwilanna's childhood, the truth about Guinevere's origins, and a rather unusual (to put it mildly!) finale. . . .

In the Last Dragon Chronicles we meet, respectively, squirrels, polar bears, monks, alien thought-beings, darklings, firebirds, and skogkatts (not to mention a unicorn or two). If you like any or all of these, you'll probably like these stories. And it might go without saying that these books are certainly for you if you can't get enough of:

DRAGONS!

9. WHISTLERS, WASTRELS, AND WOEBEGONES*

If you ask Chris what he believes the Last Dragon Chronicles is really about, he will not answer you with "squirrels," "polar bears," or even "dragons"; he will say "creativity."

Like almost every other person alive, Chris questions who he is and where he fits in this world. Unlike most people, however, he explores this through the medium of writing, "trying characters and ideas on" to see if they have any resonance. Are they *him*?

Sometimes, we have conflicting parts of ourselves that want different things — one part wanting ice cream and another part wanting Jell-O for instance. As an author, Chris cannot only have both, but also feels

---

* This is what Gwilanna disparagingly calls storytellers.

no personal conflict about it, as his characters do the wanting for him. His characters are, in truth, facets of his own self, held up to the light for examination. Thus, in these books, Chris is actually exploring his own psyche.

ANYTHING IS POSSIBLE

Chris has found, like any other author, that in a story he can be whoever he wants, do whatever he wants, and go wherever he wants, with no boundaries and no limits. Another human being? An animal? A tree? A nail in a floorboard? No problem: Anything is possible. It is relatively easy for him to describe polar bears, for example, as he knows what they look like. But the trick to being a great writer is to go beyond that and "become" that bear. To describe its thoughts, feelings and actions from the inside, as it lives them itself.

This is what Chris likes to do; in fact, he claims that if he were to be an animal, a polar bear is exactly what he would choose to be. His love and respect for them is clear in the stories.

The creation of the character David Rain, who is based on Chris as a young man, allows Chris to take a look at himself from a distance, and decide whether he likes what he sees. If not, it can all be changed.

Creating characters, in general, is a way to look at yourself, your life, your beliefs, your feelings, safely and without fear of being laughed at or ridiculed. After all, it's not *you*, is it? For young people, it's possible to test things out through someone you've created, before committing yourself to those things in real life. Not sure whether you'd enjoy being a doctor?

David Rain . . . sometimes

Write about one, and see. Feeling awkward about talking to your mom about something? Try it out on paper first.

When he was a boy, Chris always dreamed of being a rock star, a professional soccer player, or an astronaut. Needless to say, none of those things happened — he didn't want them enough. These days, he still likes to write songs but only watches soccer on TV (it requires less energy, he says). Taking a ride in the space shuttle remains a dream, but now, as a writer, he could easily experience any of those childhood fancies at the touch of a key.

David Rain starts out as a naïve, innocent young man, with a clean slate as far as his ideas about himself and his world are concerned. He has none, really. But over the course of a little more than six years, booktime, he goes on a staggering personal journey to become something beyond his wildest imaginings. Something he didn't even know it was possible to be (read the books to find out exactly what). Through writing the Last Dragon Chronicles, Chris's life, too, has changed and expanded, often beyond his own expectations. He's very grateful to his alter ego, David Rain.

INSPIRATION

Since becoming a writer (of songs and stories) the one question Chris has wrangled with is this: Where does inspiration come from? The creation of Gadzooks as a character was meant to answer that. Gadzooks is the physical manifestation of the fire within, the creative force that resides within us all. Gadzooks represents that part of us that does have all the answers — if only we could access them. Zookie, as he is affectionately called, enables David to do just that. As long as he trusts his faithful dragon and the words he writes on his pad, all is well — eventually!

The crucial thing in the stories that is emphasized repeatedly is that David *loves* Gadzooks, that he must never make him cry, so that he won't shed his fire tear, or lose his spark. In other words, David must keep Zookie's inner flame alight. In day-to-day terms, Chris is telling himself to "stay friends" with his creative source, or he will run the risk of losing its help, and with it the ability to be inspired. Believing in Gadzooks "raises his auma," that is, makes the connection to David stronger. The more that happens, the easier the connection is maintained. Self-belief is vital for a writer.

Gadzooks is also a vehicle to open David's mind to possibilities beyond those that would usually be considered the accepted norm. Likewise, by following his own intuition, Chris can create his own pathway through the world, literary or otherwise, instead of simply retracing the old familiar tracks of habit.

As if all that wasn't enough, Zookie is able to predict the future — only a very short while ahead — *or* he makes the future happen, or perhaps a little of both. In the book, it is deliberately kept ambivalent as to whether fiction is mirroring life, or vice versa. Chris is telling himself that circumstances are not always definitely one thing or another. Sometimes they are much more complex than that; wisdom often lies in keeping an open mind.

THE CREATIVE PROCESS

Chris often finds vital bits of information for a story just popping up at the exact moment he needs them. This happens far too many times to ignore. He now just accepts it as part of the creative process. And if the information isn't close to hand, a quick request to the Universe (that is, a mental plea sent out for help) usually brings what is required, and often from very unlikely sources.

Chris trusts Gadzooks in the sense that he often doesn't know what he's writing about until after he's done it. To paraphrase David, when he describes writing his stories to Liz, "It's a bit like being on a mystery tour. . . . You sort of know that you're going, but you can't be sure where until you arrive."

Chris will write anywhere. (Not on walls in subways, of course.) When away from home, he has to make do with any odd moment that he can find, at any time of day, or even night, sometimes, to type on his laptop. Ideally, however, Chris writes in the mornings, till around two-thirty if "in the zone." An average of 500–1,000 words is considered to be a "good" day — but on a "bad" day, he'll stare at the carpet till ten, cut his fingernails for fifteen minutes, and decide it's imperative that he rearrange his paper clips (individually) for another hour. Then he'll have a change of pace and strum his guitar, waiting for inspiration to come. Clearly, though, it's inspiration's day off: It will take Chris forty-three minutes and twenty-two seconds to realize this. (He'll be watching the hands of the clock by now.) Eventually, he will write a paragraph. Rewrite it. Erase some of it. Replace it in a different order. Erase all of it. Snarl a bit. Growl a bit. Write it again. Then he'll come downstairs having achieved nothing but an oversized headache. Thankfully, days like these are few and far between.

However, on those days when he does get "in the zone" — lost in that other world — he can hardly get the words out quickly enough. The story flows and pours out of him almost faster than he can write it down. Chris says this is the biggest "high" in the world. Time ceases to exist for him, and even when he comes downstairs for something to eat he is still in a daze and has to take time out to readjust to this world. It is almost as if the story has already been written on some other plane of existence, and Chris is just "listening" and copying it down; as if the story itself is a living entity and wants to be told, just as much as Chris wants to tell it. It's a cooperative venture, he says.

Other authors have spoken of a similar feeling, that they have to just "reach up" and grab a story "out of the ether." This could explain why many books on a particular subject (say, vampires, wizards, or dragons) are created at similar times. Some writers will be just "jumping on the bandwagon" of something that has been proven to be a recent commercial success, but discounting that, there is a definite "zeitgeist" (meaning "spirit of the time") effect going on. A basic idea seems to make itself known to any who are able to perceive it "floating around," but each person filters it through their own personality and writing style, so different authors will have different "takes" on it, and thus will turn out different books, all with the same theme.

Chris is interested in many different subjects beyond the boundaries of accepted reality, and explores them in his writing. Subjects such as quantum mechanics, time (is there such a thing?) travel, probable realities, parallel universes (are there other versions of "us"?), life (with or without physical bodies) on other worlds, and the expansion of consciousness all appeal to him hugely. He has always had an attraction to such topics and investigates them in his imagination before including them in his fiction. But is it fiction? Could it be that we *do* choose our own parents, as Alexa does, or that death *is* "just another place to be"? Can we heal ourselves simply by the power of thought? Or affect the outcome of situations just by intention?

Our understanding of this world is changing all the time, and there are a larger and larger numbers of scientists who are now beginning to think that some, if not all, of these things may be within our capabilities as human beings, at some point in the future, if not currently (some say there is only an eternal "now"). Perhaps in days or years or centuries to come, extrasensory perception — things like telepathy, manifesting by visualization, conversing with flowers and the apparently inanimate Universe — will be commonplace. Perhaps there really is a fine line between what you imagine and what you create. In which case, we had all better start imagining wonderful things — and thus do our part toward creating a wonderful world in which to live in peace and harmony. As David Rain says, "All things are possible with The Fire Eternal," the most creative force in the Universe.

10. ONLINE

Most authors have a Web site these days; Chris is no exception. In fact, he actually has two. The main site is www.scholastic.com/LastDragonChronicles and it has all kinds of information about the books. There are tons of facts about the series and characters along with games and activities. You can find out more about Chris here. Chris also has his own Web site, www .icefire.co.uk, that was created by Marshall Pinsent at www.pinsentdesign.com, virtually (ha!) from scratch. Chris gave him all the info, of course, but the rest was entirely Marsh's brainchild.

On this site, you can find out lots about Chris and his books, as well as a link to dragon-maker extraordinaire Valerie Chivers. Chris's Web site is also home to

Gadzooks's own literary output, a blog called Zookie's Notepad. You can find it on the Web at http://zookiesnotepad.blogspot.com. Zookie updates this each Sunday, and it usually contains tales of delight or of woe regarding the doings and failings of Chris himself, whom Zookie calls "the author." He occasionally puts paw to pencil to mention "Mrs. Author," too, usually representing me in a rather better light than Chris, for some reason.

He thinks Chris is a bit too slow on the uptake sometimes, often ignores what he has written on his pad, and even misses the fact that it is *his* genius that makes the books what they are. He's also a bit miffed that Snigger the squirrel got a handsome royalty of ten percent (paid in nuts) when *The Fire Within* came out, yet he, Zookie, has seen nary a bean for all his efforts. Maybe that's why he was so delighted when I told him he was to have his picture published.

Along with hints and tips for budding writers, the Icefire Web site also houses Chris's contact details. Fans are welcome to write to him here, and anyone looking

Gadzooks in superstar mode; pad and pencil aside, for once

to book an event with Chris can also approach him via this site. Don't forget, though, that he lives in England, which is rather a long way from America for a single school or library visit! You'll also find a list of frequently asked questions — and some of Chris's songs that relate to the books, more about those in chapter 11.

Chris receives between one hundred and two hundred e-mails a week from fans all over the world. He does his very best to answer each one individually, though this is occasionally difficult to do when he is away traveling or deep in the homestretch of book-writing. Very rarely he'll send a generic response letter, but he dislikes doing so quite intensely. He believes that if a fan has taken the trouble to write to him, then he should do them the honor of replying personally. Ages of fans range from eight to eighty-eight (to our definite knowledge) and the messages cover a whole spectrum from a simple "I think your dragon books are the best!" to great missives that are almost books in their own right. All are gratefully received. As Chris says, it is only by this kind of feedback that you know you're doing a good job — or not.

Although the majority of e-mails are from young people, a growing number are from adults, often thanking Chris for his books from a parent's point of view. These are the ones where a child with severe dyslexia, for instance, has improved because they couldn't wait for their mom or dad to read them the next installment of the story, so have picked it up themselves and persisted through their difficulties, as they just *had* to know what happened next. It is life-changing for Chris, as well as the child concerned, when he reads messages like these. The satisfaction is enormous, both on a creative level, and simply as a human being.

Some of the e-mails are incredibly funny, whether intentionally or not. Like the young lad who wrote to Chris thanking him for coming to talk at his school, saying how much he'd enjoyed the visit, and how Chris had "expired" him. We assume he meant "inspired," as we have had no visits from the local police force regarding "death by reading *Icefire*."

Another lamented the fact that he could not see and converse with dragons; his school did not have a language class in dragontongue. . . .

Chris once put a picture of his breakfast bowl up on his site; no particular reason — the camera was just handy when he was having his cereal, so he thought, *Why not?* You would not believe the amount of e-mail traffic that caused. Everyone and his sister wanted to know what was in the bowl. Even teachers were writing in, saying they had been taking bets on it being this cereal or that one. Just what is all that about? And no, I'm not telling you what brand it was. We might just be inundated.

Chris recalled reading about a famous pop star in the 1960s being quoted in an interview as liking Jelly Babies (a type of British candy). The star had sackloads sent to him by adoring fans over the next five years. Every time the interview appeared in a different paper or magazine, another batch would arrive. Although Chris doesn't go so far as to imagine he has even one *adoring* fan, he quite enjoys the idea of mentioning that he likes licorice, and fruit and nut chocolate — just in case.

And while we're on the subject of the 1960s, one bright spark asked Chris if he liked the Beatles. Thinking that he had acquired some strange sort of telepathic link with said child, he replied, "Why yes, how clever of you to realize. Indeed I do." Immediately came back the response, "Thought so. All *old* people like the Beatles. . . ." Oops. That didn't go down too well in d'Lacey-world.

We had one message from a boy who told Chris endless information about himself; where he lived, who he lived with, what their names, habits, and hobbies were; what his ambitions were; on and on. It was actually quite interesting. But right at the end of page four or thereabouts, he finished up with a final sentence:

"What was your favorite swimming stroke at school?"

It had absolutely nothing to do with the bulk of the e-mail, and left us both mystified, speechless, and then hysterical with laughter, in that order.

Chris does have some quite "normal" fan mail, in case you think he just attracts the rather strange kind. "Were you good at writing when you were at school?" is a common question. The answer is yes — and no. Take a look at Chris's school report, pictured. The real one actually read, "Chris's grammar is outstanding, but sadly this boy *does not have a creative thought in his head*." Chris was dropped down a flight of stairs when he was a baby; it obviously took thirty years for the concussion to wear off! Either that, or his creative ideas were in his socks all the time. You will also note that

Geography	Has yet to learn that one cannot eat one's dinner off a tectonic plate.	J.G.
English	... this boy does not have a creative thought in his head.	E.H
Chemistry	Progress at last. d'Lacey has only tried to blow up the lab once this term.	S.y

See me afterward, boy!

he was terrible at Geography, too. That is precisely why he made David a Geography student. Just as well he did, because it was a very useful and believable way to get our hero to the Arctic — on a field trip for college.

The "short and sweet" questions are great fun. Often an e-mail will come in with no mention of the books, and with only a dozen or so words in the message: "Describe yourself in three words" (*tall, daft, and handsome*); "Why should I get my mom to buy me a Pennykettle dragon?" (*They warm the place up, make toast in a flash — albeit a bit blackened — and reheat a cup of tea quicker than any microwave.*) "Who would you give your last Rolo to?" (*Gadzooks*); "What was your first job?" (*Screwing the handles onto coffins —* Chris's granddad was an undertaker — *then later working in a toilet paper factory — as a tester* . . . of the perforations, of course. What did you think he meant?); "If David is based on you, do you say *tee-hee-hee* and *crikey*, like David does?' (*Yes, I do* — I can vouch for this; he also snores just like David is described as doing); "What is your perfect sandwich?" (*Lancashire cheese with loads of brown sauce — but as a child: peaches, French fries, sugar, and licorice torpedos —* it is unclear whether Chris meant separately, or as one almighty mélange. And I honestly haven't had the courage to ask him. *Far* too much information.)

There was one question, however, that begged to be answered in more detail, which was "What are your top ten favorite sentences or moments that you have written in the books?" This had Chris scratching his head for a while, but here is how he responded:

1. I've always liked the tension between Bergstrom and David. It first begins in *Icefire* when David asks Bergstrom, "Who are you? Really?" and Bergstrom rather spookily replies, "Your destiny." That set the tone between them for the whole series, which is carried right through to the final chapter of *The Fire Ascending*.

2. Gretel is one of my favorite dragons. It's not always the things she says that make me laugh, but the things she does. I like the way she constantly teases those around her and dismisses the other Pennykettle dragons as useless or stupid. The one incidence of her behavior that always makes me smile is when she tries to blow smoke rings through Bonnington's ears to see if they'll come out on the other side. Poor Bonners. He never did quite get the upper paw.

3. As fans will know, a lot of scenes in the early books are set in the Arctic. I've never been to the Arctic so I have to rely on images I've seen on TV or in books

to describe it. It's always very satisfying when you come up with a line that seems to encapsulate the beauty of the place or the wildness of it. In this example from *Fire Star*, David is quoting Anders Bergstrom's description of the tundra — that hard sheet of barren permafrost that edges much of the Canadian High Arctic. Zanna and David are driving across it in a truck when David says:

"When we first arrived, I asked Bergstrom how I could describe the tundra. 'The unshaved face of God,' he called it."

The truck took a slight uneven bounce. "Well, next time you see Our Lord in Heaven, tell him to shave more often," said Zanna.

4. Zanna has come out with many great lines over the course of the series and is usually at her best when she's arguing with David. The one that always makes me shiver is in *Dark Fire* when David tells her that Alexa is destined to be an angel, a symbol of harmony

for the entire human race, and Zanna replies, *"Where on the curriculum of motherhood was this?"* It's just the perfect icy, sassy response. Ooh, she's fantastic!

5. All the principal female characters are strong and I couldn't put together a list like this without involving Lucy and Liz. Fans who wrote to me after the early books loved and loathed Lucy in equal measure. Some found her charming, others plain irritating. My favorite word to describe her was "truculent." It means "cruel or scathingly harsh," though I would tone that down to "belligerent" in her case. My favorite bit of "truculence" comes when she's a teen in *Dark Fire* and she's deliberately ignored her mom's attempts to call her. When asked to explain herself, Lucy pulls out a pair of earphones and says, *"The god that is Pod called louder. Sorry."* Moms, you've probably been there. . . .

6. And what of that super, unflappable mom, Liz Pennykettle? My favorite line of hers comes from *The*

Fire Within, when she puts the entire theme of the series into perspective. One wet and miserable day, David is stomping about the house, fed up because he's got writer's block. When Liz suggests Gadzooks might help, David says he's banished the writing dragon to the bookshelf (from the windowsill Zookie loves). When Liz queries the wisdom of this, David says:

"He's made of clay . . . He doesn't know the difference between a bookcase and a windowsill."

Elizabeth Pennykettle bristled noticeably. "Well, if that's what you think of him, no wonder he won't help you."

What she's basically saying — to all you writers out there — is never dismiss your source of inspiration, no matter how strange that may appear to be.

7. The next choice is really for Jay. When you write a major series like this you need to have a clear idea of your characters, particularly how they act and

speak, but also how they dress. David was pretty easy to visualize because he's based on me. The coat he wears in the early books came straight out of my youthful wardrobe. The interesting thing was dressing him in styles of clothing that I would have liked to have worn but never did. In *Dark Fire*, he comes into the kitchen to meet Zanna wearing a battered black coat — a kind of gunslinger look. Jay begged me to go out and purchase the same outfit! But what works at twenty-five, doesn't always translate at fifty-something.

8. My next choice is an opening line, which gives you a one in seven chance of guessing right! It actually comes from the final book, *The Fire Ascending*. When I first began to write, I tried some short stories. Any writer will tell you that the short story form seems easy, but actually requires a lot of skill. One really good tip I was given was to begin the story with a line that tells the reader something about the story as a whole. At the beginning of *The*

Fire Ascending, I had such a line. It's very simple, but very powerful: *I was a boy of twelve when I watched a dragon die.* That single line spawned the whole 20,000 words or so of Part One of the book.

9. The penultimate example is also from *The Fire Ascending* and everybody's favorite villainess, Gwilanna. No list would be complete without her involvement. Most of her remarks are pretty scathing, of course, and I could have picked lots of moments that have defined her wonderful character. But the one I really like, and that actually makes me cry whenever I read it, comes toward the end of *The Fire Ascending* when Gwilanna has finally turned to the good. She walks over to the dead polar bear Kailar, grips his ear, and offers him back the fire tear of Gawain, and she says, *"Here you are, ice bear, this is for you. Let me be an angel once in my life."* We all deserve one chance of redemption, and this is hers.

10. And for my favorite moment in the whole series I turn to *Fire World* and the wonderful librarium, that fantastic store of books on Co:pern:ica that I'm sure must keep a set of the Last Dragon Chronicles, carefully guarded by firebirds! So often throughout the series, I've found myself drawing topical issues from the news into the books. While I was writing *Fire World*, a debate was raging about whether e-books would finally replace real books (or "tree" books as people wittily call them). Having been brought up in the computer generation, I can see the argument for both. But clever as modern phones and tablets are, I don't think anything will ever provide the same sense of connection to a story or its writer that a paper book does. The librarium, with its endless floors of reading material, is a giant statement in favor of the book. And though its disorganized shelves could in no way compare to the power and speed of today's Internet, all wisdom is there nevertheless. More important, that body of

wisdom reaches out beyond the librarium, because it's not just knowing how to source knowledge that matters, it's what you do with it once acquired. It's what you create from what you learn that adds more floors to the building — ad infinitum. This is why David and Rosa find it so hard to reach the roof. It's all summed up in one fantastic line from Mr. Henry, the librarium curator. When asked by Rosa, "What's it like up there? What can you see?" he replies, "Everything. All the world can be seen from the roof of the librarium." If you don't believe that, ask a librarian. . . .

◆ ◆ ◆

Phew! That simple query nearly created a story in its own right.

Very impressive — but for me there are two questions that stand out from all the thousands of those that Chris has been asked. The first is:

"Where do you want your ashes scattered when you die?"

As it happened, Chris had a ready (and truthful) answer — the library gardens in Bromley — but for sheer originality that conversation-stopper certainly gets its inquirer ten out of ten.

The question in the second one was straightforward enough:

"If you went to a desert island, who or what would you leave behind?"

But it stands out more for Chris's reply:

"A misleading note giving my incorrect whereabouts."

Perhaps it was just one question too many that day.

11. ALL FIRED UP

One of the great advantages of being an author is being able to meet the fans as well as just hear from them by letter or e-mail. Chris used to love signing autographs, and in the dim and distant past would practice his signature endlessly (or so it seemed) in hopes of "just once" being asked to sign a book or two. Time and circumstances have changed, and now he gets writer's cramp just thinking about it. The record for the most number of books signed in a single session currently stands at around seven hundred, I believe.

In these numbers, Chris will only sign his name, but if he has the time he will also add a dedication — the person's name and a short message, too. Incidentally, we found out that a book signed by the author but with no other wordage added is more valuable than one signed *to* someone.

The only exception here, apparently, is if there is what is called "good provenance" in a dedication. This means that if the book was signed to someone who was famous in their own right, say, and it could be proven that the dedication was genuine, then that would be worth more than a book with the author's signature alone. Of course, a personal message is always worth more to the individual than any monetary value that could be put upon it, and quite rightly so. Chris has twice signed books with messages in a foreign language: German and Welsh. He had to learn them deliberately before he started, but the recipients were surprised and delighted.

And while we're on the subject, the Last Dragon Chronicles are themselves available in a number of different languages. The countries where translated editions are published include Germany, Romania, the Czech Republic, Hungary, Brazil, and Japan.

The dragon books are incredibly popular in the

United States. Chris now wishes he had tacked a map of that country up on the wall, so he could stick a pin in for every state that he's had an e-mail from. He thinks it must be every single one by now. It would certainly seem so, as the series has consistently appeared on the *New York Times* bestseller lists.

The foreign editions are beautiful creations. Some have a few black and white line drawings in them, but the Japanese versions are especially awesome. As well as line drawings, they also have full-color illustrations at the front of the book. Or rather, the "back" of the book, as we would perceive it, since the Japanese language is written in ideographs (glyphs or "pictures") and read from top to bottom and right to left, in columns. So starting in the top-right corner, you read down the rightmost column first, then go back up to the top of the page and read the next left column till you get to the bottom of the page again, and so on. Thus you would appear to be reading the book backward when compared to the way we are used to in the west.

The Fire Within –
Czech Republic

Icefire – *Germany*

Fire Star – *Japan*

The Fire Eternal – *UK*

All the translations for foreign editions are done in the country of publication (Chris is ace at English and passable in dragontongue and felinespeak, but useless at any other languages), and according to friends who have read the books in their own native language and in English, they are pretty faithful to the originals. Translations do not seem to pose too much of a barrier for those doing them, except that once Chris had a frantic e-mail from the Japanese translator, desperate to know what "daft as a brush" meant. The complicated plotlines and esoteric mysticisms were easy-peasy, allegedly, but that one had them stumped. Colloquial English is a tricky idiom to explain, even for the English native speaker, and Chris did his best, but he'd love to know how that phrase was expressed, in the end.

THE DRAGONS OF
WAYWARD CRESCENT

Chris also wrote a spinoff series from the original novels, for younger readers mainly, though it seems all age groups (including adults) are enjoying them, from the feedback received. Each book features one of the Pennykettle dragons and tells the story of its creation and its own special ability.

The two books currently published are about Gruffen and Gauge, both of whom appear in the Last Dragon Chronicles series. The Wayward Crescent books are meant as a prequel to *The Fire Within*, as they are all set in the Pennykettle household before David arrives as their tenant. They also fill in a lot of background history to the Pennykettles and their dragons, which is what has piqued the interest of some people from older age groups.

THE SONGS

Chris has also recorded a couple of songs relating to the Last Dragon Chronicles. Called "Fire Star" and "The Fire Eternal," they can be found on Chris's Web site (www.icefire.co.uk), but as yet they are not available to download (though this may change if any record companies take an interest!). All instruments are played by Chris, and all the vocals are his, too, but sung from David's point of view. The lyrics are as follows, for those of you who are interested:

"Fire Star"
There is a sign in the heavens
Another light in the darkness
A better time is beginning
There is a fire star coming

I see the mark of the ice bear
In the tears of the dragon
And you'd better start wishing
There is a fire star coming

Stay with me, my love. . . .

There is a sign in the heavens
Another light in the darkness
And you'd better start wishing
There is a fire star coming

"The Fire Eternal"

It's like breathing in several degrees of the sun
The ice and the fire all rolled into one
And look at the shape of the man you've
  become
It ain't easy, touching the sky
It ain't easy, learning to die
It ain't easy, stepping outside of the circle
Into the Fire Eternal

How could you think this is all we were worth?
My love for you beats at the heart of the Earth
I was around with the stars at their birth
It ain't easy, turning the page
It ain't easy, taking the stage
It ain't easy, facing the final rehearsal
Before the Fire Eternal

And, hey, what you thought was finality
Preys on your fears of mortality
Here, in this changing reality world

Stand on the edge of the light with me
Take in the wonders of flight with me
in this calling, truth and love are one . . . om

Atoms and dust at the core of your star
But what you perceive here is not what you are
The journey to wisdom is not very far
It ain't easy, taking the stage
It ain't easy, turning the page
It ain't easy, stepping outside of the circle
Into the Fire Eternal
Into the Fire Eternal
Love is the Fire Eternal. . . .

The first line of the "Fire Eternal" lyric was inspired by a line David speaks in *Dark Fire*, in response to a question that Zanna asks.

Chris also has several other songs, unrelated to the Last Dragon Chronicles, posted on the Internet at www.myspace.com/chrisdlacey.

◆ ◆ ◆

And for those few of you who have been astute enough to notice the dots at the beginning and end of the poem at the conclusion of the third book, *Fire Star*, yes, that does mean that the published lines are only a snippet of a longer piece. They are an abridged (and slightly adapted) version of a poem Chris wrote, again from David's point of view, called "G'lant." G'lant is an invisible dragon, given to Zanna by David when he has been pierced through the heart with a spear of ice. For the first time in print, here it is in full:

"G'lant"
That night I gave you a Valentine dragon,
a fissure opened deep within the Earth
and all below me tilted. Frosted crystals
chimed the air, melting on your tender kiss
as all your warmth and bliss came mine,
for one degree of sway, of time.

On that beat, my heart struck up
a plangent chord and drew
whatever magma rose to light
that single shining spark within
your dark, breathtaking eyes.
So brown, so like the Earth herself.
This moving ground, this slanted shelf.

Here is my quest, my pledge to you:
that life and all its tangled plights
could not call down a single wake
to quench this dragon's winter task.
Until the stars have blinked their last,
wherever on this Earth you walk,
he will arouse, excite, inspire,
and keep alight that spark,
this fire.

THE LAST WORD

I trust you've found this ramble through the Last Dragon Chronicles and its author's life entertaining and informative, but I really can't finish this book without a last word from Gadzooks — which is, of course, *hrrr.* . . .

A Q&A WITH
CHRIS D'LACEY

Which is your favorite character in the series?

I usually split this up into two categories — human and dragon. Let's deal with the human first. It's very hard for me not to choose David, as he is based on me when I was a young man. If the series had gone no further than *Fire Star*, I probably would have chosen him. Of course, there are many characters I could opt for. Gwilanna has been fantastic to write — villains always are. And Anders Bergstom intrigues me as much now as he ever did in *Icefire*. But the human I really like is Zanna (and her "alternative" in *Fire World*, Rosa). She has a lot to deal with throughout the series. I love her spirit, particularly the way she copes with David's disappearance in *The Fire Eternal*. And she's a great mum. I would have loved to have met her when I was David's age!

As for the dragons. I'm in danger of being seriously scorched, here, by the ones I leave out. Seriously, I love them all. They make me laugh and cry in equal measure. Sentiment says I should pick Grace, because she will probably never get over having her ears broken by David. In the end, if I'm forced into a corner, it comes down to two. Gretel is just brilliant. Her feistiness, especially in *Icefire*, is legendary. I like the way you can never be quite sure about her and how she thinks the other Pennykettle dragons are "useless." But even she would forgive me for choosing the one and only Gadzooks as my favorite. How could a writer not choose the writing dragon? Notice that *The Fire Ascending* is dedicated to him. That just about says it all.

Which is your favorite book in the series?

Again, very, very difficult to choose. For a long time I would have picked *The Fire Within*, because it's not a book about squirrels and it's not a book about dragons; it's a book about creativity and where ideas come from — a subject close to a writer's heart. When I wrote *Dark Fire*, that took over as my favorite for a while. It has so many lovely twists and turns and it was great to write about Gawaine, the queen dragon, coming out of stasis. Then came *Fire World*, and my feelings changed again. At the end of *Dark Fire*, I knew I had to come up with something spectacular to explain the ending at Scuffenbury Hill. It was a real gamble to dive into the alternative world of Co:pern:ica, but, boy, was it good fun! A small number of readers just didn't get it. But those that did couldn't praise it enough. I absolutely adore *Fire World*. I don't think it's the best book of the series, but it is my favorite — just.

So which book *is* the best of the series for you?

The Fire Ascending, without a doubt. It wraps everything up so beautifully. Again, I took risks. I knew I wanted to go back in time and examine the story

273

of Guinevere and Gawain, but I wasn't expecting to write a 20,000 word chunk of prehistory without any chapter breaks that didn't include any of the known characters (or barely any) and introduced a villain we hadn't met before! That spirit of adventure set the tone for the rest of the book. It was just a question then of how to mix the old with the new and bring everything to a satisfying conclusion. I think *The Fire Ascending* contains some of the best bits of writing I've ever done.

Where did you get your character names from? Are they made up or did you choose any of them in homage to anything else?

The only two characters that weren't entirely made up are David and Zanna. David is a name I've always liked and wouldn't have minded being called. Zanna came about after I met a girl at a signing who called herself that. She was a Goth and very striking. I asked her if "Zanna" was an Eastern European name, to which she replied, "No, it's short for Suzanna, you . . ." I won't repeat the rest! I thought it was such a cool name and immediately wrote it into *Icefire*. Nearly all the other names, including Gadzooks, just floated into my consciousness when their character was first introduced. It rarely takes me more than a minute to find something I like or that seems appropriate. And the character will soon tell you if the name is wrong; they dig their heels in and refuse to be written. I was really struck with Ingavar (the polar bear), because it conjures up an image of a hugely powerful and courageous bear. It was always good fun making up names for the Inuit characters. Tootega was my favorite. Voss was interesting. I wanted to give the opening section of *The Fire Ascending* a vaguely Scandinavian feel. I typed "Norway" into Google and one of the first words I saw was "Voss" (an area of Norway). I liked it and it stuck. Henry Bacon, I have to confess, is a slight homage to Mr. Curry, the annoying neighbor in the Paddington Bear books. Curry? Bacon? See the connection? Many people have asked if the use of the names Gawain,

Guinevere, and Arthur is some kind of nod to the Arthurian legends. No, not at all. I just liked the sound of them. Gawain, particularly, is a wonderful title for a dragon.

When did you know how the series was going to end? Did you plan it from near the beginning?

There's an old saying that goes, "every story is as long as it needs to be." I don't think anyone quite expected seven books at a time when trilogies were all the rage, but I always felt that if the story was there I would be happy to continue adding to the series. I did consider writing *The Fire Ascending* as two books, where book one would have dealt with the historical stuff (Agawin, Grella, etc.) and book two the Ix inversion. But after a little discussion with my editors we felt that one volume would be enough. I did cut out a long history of Co:pern:ica, and I would have seriously liked to have dedicated more chapters to Gwilanna's illumination to Gawain. But I'd rather people have a book, not a doorstop. I'm happy with the way things worked out. As for the ending, would you believe I didn't know the exact ending until a few days before I wrote it? I decided from the start (well, from *Icefire* onward) that I would write these books "organically." In other words, I wouldn't plan them at all but would just let them take me wherever they wanted to go, to keep them "true" to what David does when he writes *Snigger and the Nutbeast* for Lucy. With every book, I always knew what the beginning would be, and I had a *vague* idea of the ending. Everything in between was an adventure! It's a scary way to write, but for me it's the only real way to do it. I placed my faith in the Universe — and let Gadzooks do the rest! Of course, there is a great responsibility on a writer to wrap up a big series in a satisfactory manner. I'm well known for leaving dreadful cliffhangers at the end of my books. I couldn't allow that to happen with *The Fire Ascending*. It had to have a definite end and it had to be good, but more than that, it had to be different. I came up with the idea of the interview sequence before I started the book, but didn't tell anyone except Jay about it until it was done. I'm absolutely thrilled with the way it came out. It puts the whole series into perspective and is both funny and moving in equal measure. The closing lines didn't really come to me until very near the end. What I like about them is how they address the two main themes of the series, i.e., the power of the mind to create ideas and whether dragons exist — or not.

What have been the highs and lows of the series?

It's been a delight to unwrap so much wonderful story. As I said above, when you write the way I do you're never quite sure what's going to happen. So it's really exciting when fantastic scenes pop up out of nowhere. Developing the covers has been another thrill. Angelo (Rinaldi) has done a fabulous job with the artwork, which has become iconic. My favorite cover is *The*

Fire Eternal (love the planet in the eye), closely followed by *Fire World*. Someone jokingly suggested that I couldn't write any more books because we've run out of colors! Pink dragon, anyone? Maybe not. If I had a low at all, it would be the feeling that over a period of years, books like these tend to be taken for granted. People see three, four, five come out and assume they know what they're getting. My answer to that would be, read *Fire World*. How many series take a complete sideways step, six books in, and manage to pull it off? I'm sometimes told as well that the plots are confusing or complicated. Yes, they are, probably because of the way the books are written. And maybe it's partly due to the fact that my two favorite television series were *The X Files* and *Twin Peaks*, which had so many layers of intrigue that it was virtually impossible to finish them conclusively. I learned a lesson there. I think *The Fire Ascending* does have a strong conclusion, one which brings the whole series together.

What will you miss most about writing the series?

I've lived with these characters for over ten years. It's going to seem odd not writing about them. I've always felt happy in Wayward Crescent and will miss visiting the kitchen at number 42. I can see Bonnington at his food bowl as I type this. More than anything, I will miss the Pennykettle dragons. Their innocence and humor and occasional mischievous behavior was always a joy to experience. I used to believe I was better at writing domestic dramas than full-on fantasy. Part one of *The Fire Ascending* has changed my mind about that. But although I could see me writing another book about dragons, it almost certainly wouldn't be about *those* dragons. There is a degree of sadness about that. But no matter what else I do, I will always be associated with David, Gadzooks, and the Dragons' Den, which is fine by me. They have made me what I am and I would miss telling their stories at school visits — not that they'll ever let me ignore them (they're *hurr*ing in my ear even now . . .).

What *won't* you miss?

Writing a lengthy series like this brings its own kind of pressures. To keep the momentum going, the books have to be delivered regularly. That has not always been easy. I could have written a different ending to *Dark Fire* and quit the series there, but it would have left too many unanswered questions. I could never have put the Chronicles away without feeling entirely happy about the ending. Other than that, I don't think there's anything I would miss. These books opened me up to a new genre. They have taken me to places in the world I might never have visited otherwise and brought me into contact with lots of wonderful people. But I guess the last word should go to the fans. I've had thousands of messages over the years from boys and girls (and, yes, many "grown-ups") who've told me the books are amazing and even life changing. That's a humbling feeling when you get right down to it. I want to thank them all and say I hope you enjoyed the conclusion. One day, we will get a movie (or three) for you. Then you can say you were there at the beginning, before the whole world knew the meaning of *hrrr!*

Chris d'Lacey
January 2012

ILLUSTRATION AND PHOTOGRAPHY COPYRIGHT AND PERMISSIONS

Scrubbley station sign (p. 5) © Chris d'Lacey

Housing available ad (p. 8) © Orchard Books

Anatomy of a Pennykettle Dragon (p. 22) © Chris d'Lacey, permitted for use by Val Chivers

Boley the polar bear (p. 30) © Chris d'Lacey

The Library Gardens, Scrubbley (p. 34) © Orchard Books

Val Chivers (p. 43) © Chris d'Lacey, permitted for use by Val Chivers

Nutbeast collage covers (p. 46) © Orchard Books

Nutbeast cartoon cover (p. 47) © Tania Hunt-Newton

Original fire tear design (p. 48) © Orchard Books

Unused rough for *Dark Fire* (p. 49) © Angelo Rinaldi

Line drawings from Japanese editions (p. 67, 69, 75, 76) © Take Shobo

New Walk (p. 107) © Chris d'Lacey

Conker's sanctuary (p. 109) © Chris d'Lacey

Scuffenbury in dragontongue (p. 139) © Orchard Books

Chris and Jay d'Lacey are the authors of *Rain & Fire*, a companion to the *New York Times* bestselling Last Dragon Chronicles. Chris d'Lacey is the author of many highly acclaimed novels for children and young adults, including the books in the Last Dragon Chronicles: *The Fire Within*, *Icefire*, *Fire Star*, *The Fire Eternal*, *Dark Fire*, *Fire World*, and *The Fire Ascending*. He is also the author of the early chapter books series The Dragons of Wayward Crescent. Chris and Jay are married and live in Devon, England.

To learn more about Chris d'Lacey's books visit www.scholastic.com/LastDragonChronicles.

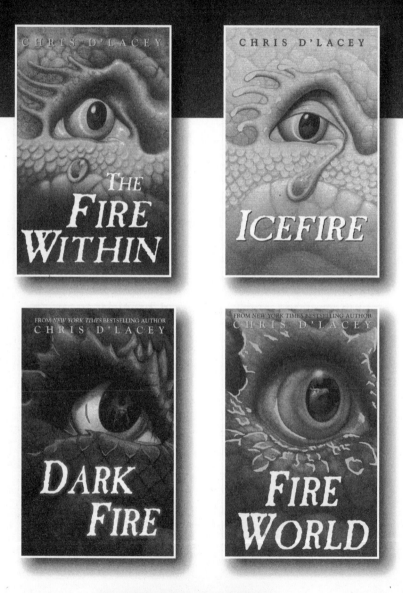

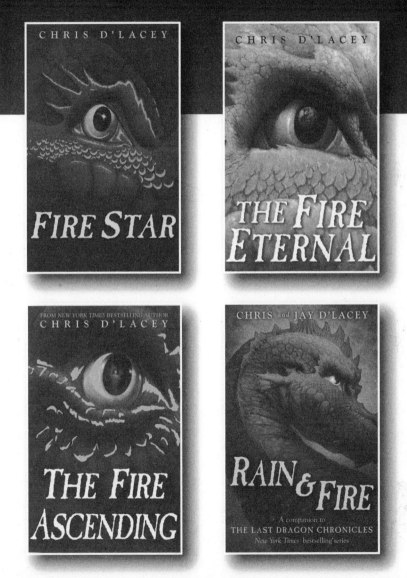